Devil in a Black Suit

Colleen Helme

Book Layout & Design ©2018 - BookDesignTemplates.com
Book Cover by Damonza ©2018 – Colleen Helme

Devil in a Black Suit/ Colleen Helme. -- 1st ed.
ISBN-13: 978-1983781193
ISBN-10: 1983781193

Dedication

To Darlene M. Mercado,
You would have loved this one
Rest in Peace

The Shelby Nichols Adventure Series

Note from the Author

This book is about Ramos, the hitman from the Shelby Nichols Adventure Series. It is a stand-alone novel from Ramos's point of view and is based on the characters from the series. For readers of the series, this book takes place between book seven, *Crossing Danger*, and book eight, *Devious Minds*. I hope you love it!

ACKNOWLEDGEMENTS

I would like to give a big thanks to my family for all of your support and encouragement. To Ben Towers who helped me with the research about the guns and weapons mentioned in this book. Now I don't have to worry about the FBI flagging me as a terrorist! Also thanks to Brian Chatwin and Geoff Parker for your insights and first-hand experiences in Cuba. Thanks again to my great editor, Kristin Monson, for making this a better book. Most of all, thanks to all of my readers who embraced the idea of a book about Ramos, and gave me the motivation to write his story! It's been a fun journey, and one that I hope will continue.

Contents

Part 1

Chapter 1

Ramos sat at the bar, waiting for Shelby and Manetto to finish up their meeting. Shelby hadn't wanted to come, and he couldn't blame her, but she didn't have much of a choice when it came to Manetto. Neither did anyone else who worked for him.

It wasn't like this was anything that could get her killed, but with Shelby, he never knew what to expect. She was a valuable asset to Manetto, the local crime boss, because she could read minds. Who would have thought? Even after a few months of working with Shelby, the fact that she could read minds still blew Ramos away.

And to think that it had all happened because she'd gone to the grocery store for some carrots. That was the day a bank robber shot her. It was the bullet wound to her head that had given her this ability. But it wasn't until Ramos had tracked her down for Manetto, that she'd told the big boss her secret.

It had given Manetto a reason to let her live, and now she was a member of his organization, even though she worked for him under duress. She even called him "Uncle Joey," mostly to make him mad, but Manetto took it all in stride, and continued to coerce her by any means necessary to do his bidding.

Since Ramos worked for him as well, it also meant that he had shared some intense moments with Shelby. In fact, he'd nearly died a few times saving her life. It even looked like he had a soft spot in his heart for her, and that irritated him more than anything.

There didn't used to be anything soft about Ramos, but with Shelby in his life, he'd changed. Of course, their relationship had never gotten physical, since she was married with boundaries he had to respect. And he was a notorious hit-man for a crime boss, so long-term relationships weren't part of his life.

Still, he liked to push her buttons as often as possible, just to see if he could wear her down. What could he say? He was one of the bad guys, and he had a reputation to uphold.

Tired of sitting, he stood, turning his back to the wall and facing the growing number of people crowded into the club. The usual Tuesday night gathering was just starting to get rowdy, and he kept a vigilant watch for anyone too interested in the room behind him where the meeting was taking place.

A group of people to his left shifted, giving him a perfect view of a beautiful woman with wavy, shoulder-length, dark hair. She glanced in his direction, and his breath caught. What the hell? She held his gaze and raised one sculpted eyebrow in a clear invitation to join her.

Ramos let out his breath. After Mexico, he thought he'd never see her again. If she was here, that meant she wanted something from him, and it couldn't be good.

Ramos sent her a nod, then caught Ricky's attention and motioned him over. After Ramos instructed Ricky to take his place standing guard, he made his way through the crowd toward the woman.

As he reached her, she inclined her head toward an empty table in the back where it wasn't as noisy. With misgiving, he nodded and followed behind, taking a seat beside her.

"It's been a while," she said, her voice just as sultry as he remembered.

Ramos nodded, allowing a rueful smile to play on his lips. "After Mexico I didn't think I'd see you again."

"No doubt," she agreed, a small smile twisting her lips. "I'm glad you made it back home safely. I even heard you caught the assassin that came after you."

He narrowed his gaze. How did she know that? "So why are you here? I thought we were even."

"Can't a girl stop by to say hello?"

"Maybe," he chuckled. "But we both know you're not that girl."

She shrugged, then shifted in her chair to get closer to him. "Let's just say I need a favor, and I would be extremely grateful if you could help me out."

"You? That surprises me. We both know you have plenty of resources without asking me for help."

"That's true. But don't forget that without my help, you might not have made it out of Mexico alive." Her dark chocolate eyes held a challenge, but he caught a glimpse of vulnerability that pricked his conscience. She was right, but he'd hoped they were even after the deal they'd made.

Several months ago, he and Manetto had gone to Mexico to find Manetto's niece, Kate, who'd double-crossed Manetto and run off with a lot of money. Naturally they'd gone after her to get it back, only to run into Manetto's old flame who needed help getting out from under a drug cartel. They'd had to take on the cartel to save her life, and the life of her son.

Manetto might not have gotten involved, except that she'd told him the boy was his son as well. To make matters worse, she told Manetto that the cartel was holding their son hostage, and things didn't look good.

After that shocking revelation, Manetto decided to take matters into his own hands. With his resources, he was willing to spend whatever it took to protect them both, even if he wasn't sure the boy was his.

That's where Sloan came in. Ramos met her the day he'd gone to the home of a known arms dealer hoping to find a few mercenaries he could trust. Sloan was there, meeting with the dealer, and looking for information on the cartel.

The moment they met, an undeniable attraction sizzled between them, hitting him like an electric charge. He'd never had a reaction like that before, and it took him by surprise. The revelation that she was interested in taking down the same cartel seemed like a twist of fate. He never dreamed that she was hiding anything. In hindsight, he should have known it was too easy, but he'd been blinded to the truth by his attraction to her.

They'd worked together night and day like a well-oiled machine. She knew things about the cartel that he didn't, and he had the resources that she lacked to buy the guns and mercenaries they needed to get the job done.

Planning everything together quickly led to a more intimate relationship. In fact, they could hardly keep their hands off each other. Their affair was both exhilarating and heady, especially given the risks they were taking and the real possibility of death. He'd never felt so free and alive before in his life.

It was only after they'd taken the cartel down that Ramos discovered the appalling truth that she was a U.S. agent. Even some of the mercenaries he'd been fighting with were part of her team, and he and Manetto had just helped them fulfill their assignment.

She'd used him. And, like a festering wound, the pain it brought was still there.

Right before he'd left Mexico, she confessed that she never could have taken down the cartel without his help, but she'd never meant to get so involved with him. He may have thought she'd used him, but she felt they'd shared something special.

That did little to appease the betrayal Ramos felt, and he'd wanted nothing more to do with her. But the damage had been done, and now the agents had both him and Manetto on their radar.

So Ramos struck a deal with her. If she really meant what she'd said and wasn't using him, she'd do everything she could to keep her agency off his back. She'd surprised him by quickly agreeing to all of his demands.

He'd had to leave Mexico in a hurry after that, because Shelby needed protection from a couple of cartel members who'd gone to the states after her. They'd discovered that Manetto had managed to pilfer several million dollars from the cartel, which he'd stashed in Shelby's bank account for safe keeping.

At home, he'd found that Sloan's people had been hounding Shelby, but once the problem had been resolved, they'd left him and Manetto alone. He'd figured that Sloan had kept her word, but he'd vowed to never get involved with her again.

Now here she was, asking for his help.

He let out a breath and glanced her way, feeling the same stirrings of desire that had held him captive from before, and found that he couldn't turn her down, at least not until he knew what she was up to.

"What do you need?" he asked. The slight relaxing of her shoulders gave away her relief that she'd gotten through to him. But he wasn't about to commit to anything yet.

"I've been tracking an arms dealer from Mexico who recently came into some information. He thinks that your boss might have a large shipment of guns and other merchandise for sale."

Ramos scowled. "You know Manetto doesn't deal in weapons."

She shrugged. "After you took down the cartel, Manetto gained a reputation. He might be the only person Carlos would be willing to risk doing business with, and Manetto got the weapons he needed to do the job, right? So it's not a stretch to believe he has connections."

"Yeah, especially if someone let it slip that he was in the market." Ramos caught her gaze and raised his brow.

"Hey...I've been after Carlos for long time, and this is my opportunity to finally catch him. It's a good set-up."

Ramos sat back in his chair, then folded his arms and let out a breath. Only Sloan would dare ask him a favor like this. "Manetto won't do it."

She stole a glance at him and nervously licked her lips. "It might be a little late for that. Carlos is already here."

Ramos swore under his breath and leaned forward. "Do you have a death wish or something?"

"It won't hurt to ask your boss," she countered. "Just remind him that neither of you would have survived in Mexico without me."

She was probably right, but Manetto didn't like being coerced, and neither did he. "I can talk to Manetto, but you have to make an offer, then I need something from you, or he won't bite."

Her gaze narrowed with annoyance. "It seems you're forgetting who I work for."

"I don't think so," he said, his voice dry. "You made that quite clear in Mexico. As I recall, we helped each other."

Their gazes locked in an angry battle, bringing with it the heat of attraction. Unbidden, the taste of her lips, and the feel of her body pressed against his rose in his memory, but he pushed the thought away. She'd used him, and the threat of exposure wasn't something he was likely to forget.

"Fine," she said. "Tell him that I'll owe him another favor."

Ramos's brows rose with surprise that she'd given in so easily. She must be desperate. "Anything?"

Her lips twisted with frustration. "Yes. Within my power."

"Okay, at least that gives me something to work with, but don't get your hopes up. I'll talk with him tonight. He's in a meeting right now, but he should be just about done if you want to wait."

Her gaze darted around the room, and she shook her head. "No. I've been here long enough." She pulled a burner phone from her pocket and handed it to him. "This is secure. I'll call you in an hour."

Before he could answer, she slipped out of her chair and her lithe form disappeared into the crowd.

Damn. Ramos let out a breath and shook his head. Given that she'd conceded so quickly to owing Manetto a favor, he had to believe that this whole operation was going down soon and fast. He didn't like that one bit. He also didn't like the heady pull of attraction he felt between them. He'd thought he was over her. Why did she have to turn up and complicate his life?

He made his way back to the bar and told Ricky to wait there, explaining that something had come up and he'd need him to take Shelby home.

It had been over an hour since the meeting had started, so he knocked on the door and glanced inside. Manetto motioned him in, then stood to indicate that the meeting was over. As Manetto continued to talk to the two men beside him, Shelby stood from her spot at the table and gave Ramos a smile. Then her brows drew together.

Ramos quickly closed off his thoughts and hoped she hadn't picked up anything. But from her frown, he wasn't sure he'd been successful.

"What's wrong?" she asked, coming to his side.

He gave her a moment to elaborate, but when she didn't, he let out a relieved breath. "Something's come up, but it's nothing for you to worry about. I just need to talk to Manetto. Are you all right if Ricky takes you home?"

Her eyes narrowed with suspicion. "Sure. But I need to tell Uncle Joey what I picked up from this meeting first."

As her gaze caught his, Ramos bolstered the barrier in his mind, something he'd learned to do around Shelby. With her mind-reading skills, it was a necessity, but one he'd used enough times that it worked pretty well. From her irritated scowl, he knew he'd succeeded.

The door closed on their visitors, and Manetto turned to face them with a smile. "That went well. Let's all sit down so Shelby can tell me what she found out."

After sitting, she began. "Well, the good news is that they're willing to do things your way, and they're grateful for the loan. But they also have a plan in place to buy you out after the first six months."

"How do they plan on doing that?" Manetto asked.

"Something about the shares," Shelby continued. "I think they're trying to buy them under an umbrella company or something? Since I don't really know what that means, it doesn't make a lot of sense to me, but I'm sure it does to you."

"Yes. I know exactly what it means. Do they have any off-shore accounts?"

Shelby shrugged. "I don't know for sure, but when you mentioned your holdings in the Caymans, one of them thought about an ocean and a man holding a steel box. Does that count?"

"Sounds like an off-shore account to me," Manetto said. "Anything else?"

"Uh...no. I think that's it."

"Good. That's very helpful, Shelby."

"Great. If that's it, I should probably get going." She glanced at her watch. "It's late."

"Oh...there's one more thing," Manetto said. "Can you swing by the office tomorrow or the next day? With Christmas next week, I want to make sure I get Jackie the right gift. Maybe you could find out what she wants the most, and let me know."

"What are you thinking of getting her?"

"She seems to like diamonds a lot...so something like earrings, or a bracelet, or a necklace...unless there's something else she'd rather have."

"Okay, I'll come by tomorrow and talk with her," Shelby agreed.

They stood to leave, and Ramos turned to Manetto. "Ricky's taking her home. Something's come up that I need to discuss with you."

Manetto's gaze narrowed, and he sent Ramos a nod. "All right. Thanks Shelby. I'll see you tomorrow."

After the door shut behind her, Manetto turned to Ramos. "What is it?"

Ramos sighed and shook his head. "Remember Sloan, the government agent who helped us in Mexico?"

"Of course."

"She just showed up here, and she wants something from us." Ramos explained the situation, not missing Manetto's cold glare and raised brows. "I told her you'd never go for it, but she said he's already here for the deal. Because of that, she said she's willing to owe us another favor if we help her out."

"A favor...well, I guess that's something." Manetto let out a breath, "Especially with Blake Beauchaine breathing down my neck."

"That's true," Ramos agreed. Blake had reconnected with Manetto about a month ago. They'd been close friends in college, but after a dispute, they had gone their separate ways, each ending up on different sides of the law. As a government agent, Blake wasn't above putting Manetto and his business under scrutiny, and it made Manetto nervous.

"So," Manetto continued. "This Carlos person is here and expecting to buy weapons from me. There might be a way to work with that. But...I'm afraid I can't be involved." He caught Ramos's gaze. "It would have to be your operation, not mine, and I'm fine if you don't want to do it."

Did Ramos really want to get involved in all this? No, but it was Sloan. She was counting on him, and he found it hard to turn her down. Not only had she risked her neck to help him out in Mexico, but they'd meant something to each other once. Maybe they still did.

"What do you think?" Manetto asked. "Are you willing to risk it?"

"Yeah," Ramos said. "I'll do it. What do you have in mind?"

Manetto smiled. "It's pretty cut and dry. Sloan supplies the weapons, Carlos pays for the weapons. We keep the payment for our troubles. It's up to her to catch the guy and get the weapons back. See? No one loses."

"Except for Carlos."

"Yeah. That's why I can't be the seller. If it got out that I turned him in to the feds, it could ruin my reputation. It could ruin yours, too. So maybe it wouldn't be so bad if Carlos didn't survive the deal, but I'll leave that little detail up to you."

Ramos nodded, wondering if he'd regret his decision. It would put him in a tight spot working with the feds, and he'd have to be careful that Sloan didn't double-cross him. Not that he thought she would, but what about her team? If they found out who he was, they might not be so inclined to look the other way.

"There's always the favor she'll owe us," Manetto said. "It might come in handy the next time Blake shows up. I know he's interested in Shelby, and that worries me. I don't want him finding out about her special talent. It's already bad enough that he believes in her 'premonitions.' If he knew the truth...I'd hate to think what would happen."

"You're right. I'll see what I can work out. Sloan is supposed to call me on this." He took the phone from his pocket. "It's a burner phone."

Uncle Joey's brows drew together. "Hmm...that means they might be monitoring our phones again. I'll have Nick get on that first thing in the morning. We'll talk about this then."

"Sounds good," Ramos agreed. "Depending on how it goes, I might want someone to watch my back."

"Use whoever you need."

Manetto left soon after that, leaving Ramos to wait at the bar for Sloan's call. It wasn't long before he felt the vibration in his pocket. "Yes?"

"I'm across the street in the apartment above the diner. Come around to the back staircase, and I'll let you in."

Ramos shook his head and pocketed the phone. So that's how she knew where he was, she'd been spying on him.

What else did she know? Too bad he didn't have Shelby's skill. It could sure come in handy right about now.

He zipped up his leather jacket against the cold and left the club. Sloan met him at the back door and motioned him inside. She had changed her clothes, wearing black tights and a tank-top under a long-sleeved cardigan, with slippers on her feet.

He climbed up the steep staircase behind her and couldn't help admiring the view. Keeping her at arm's length could be a struggle but, until he knew more, he wasn't about to make that mistake again.

She opened the door to the small apartment and led him inside. "I've got coffee. Do you want some?"

"Sure," he replied. Inside, he noted the small kitchen on one side of the apartment, and the living room with a couch on the other. As he took off his jacket, he caught sight of a tripod with a camera and telephoto lens at the window.

His breath caught, and anger bubbled in his chest that she was taking pictures of the club...and him. Then wariness replaced it. Why would she let him see this? She could have taken it down, but she wanted him to know. Was she that confident that he'd agree to her plan? She came to his side and handed him a warm mug.

"It looks like you've got a nice set-up here, with a perfect view of the club."

She shrugged. "I had to make sure you and Manetto were there. Let's sit down."

She plopped on the couch, expecting him to follow, and pulled her feet up under her. With a frown, Ramos took a seat on the other end, leery of getting too close. There was no way he would ever fully trust her, and he didn't want to fall into a trap.

"So what did Manetto say?" she asked, totally ignoring his scowl.

"He won't do it." At her indrawn breath, he waited a beat before continuing. "But he agreed that I could take over in his stead."

"Okay. That should work. They know you're his right-hand man, so that shouldn't be a problem."

"He's still holding you to your end of the bargain."

"Of course." She glanced at him with a tight smile. "Let's get started. I've been feeding Carlos information about the weapons that Manetto wants to sell. I can set it up for Carlos to come to the club to meet with Manetto, but you can meet with him instead. It might spook him a little, but there's nothing we can do about it now. Here's his photo."

She picked up a photo from the coffee table and handed it to him. He half expected to recognize the man, but there wasn't anything familiar about him, and he handed it back.

"I can arrange for him to meet with you tomorrow night, and then the two of you can set up the exchange. I was hoping to use one of Manetto's warehouses for the deal."

"Not one of Manetto's," Ramos said. "He wouldn't want anything like this to be traced back to him, but I know of an abandoned factory that will work. And before we go any further, I need to know what sorts of weapons you have."

"Sure," she said, shrugging like it was no big deal. "Carlos is in the market for rocket launchers, and I have twenty, along with the stinger missiles that go with them. Besides that, I have a few RPGs to sweeten the deal, and a couple of cases of M16's and night-vision goggles...plenty of things Carlos would pay top dollar for."

Ramos shook his head in wonder. "How did you get your hands on all of that?"

"Let's just say my superiors are loaning them to me for this operation."

"Hmm...they must want this guy pretty bad. Or you just know how to get your way."

She sent him a pleased grin. "You might say that."

Ramos admired her spunk. It was one of the things that drew him to her. And she was a lot like him, only on the good side of the law. "Pretty soon, you'll be running the place."

"Ha...not hardly, but I'm working on it."

That didn't surprise him. "All right. I can see how this might work. So where are the weapons?"

"My team is en route. They're just waiting for the go ahead from me."

"I see." It looked like she'd been planning this whole operation for quite some time. She must have been pretty sure he'd agree, and that bothered him. What else did she have up her sleeve? Sure, Manetto was a prime candidate to sell the weapons, but someone undercover could have worked just as well.

She lowered her gaze and took a sip of her coffee. "We can go over our strategy tomorrow morning, and you can show me this abandoned factory of yours."

She leaned back against the cushion, smiling at him invitingly. Her sweater fell off her shoulder, exposing the beautiful curve of her neck. It brought back all those memories of their time together, and he realized she wanted that again.

Part of him wanted her, too. But even though the attraction was still there, he wasn't about to get pulled into her schemes. Who knew what else she'd want from him then? No one ever did anything for anyone without wanting something in return...except for maybe Shelby.

Ignoring her heated gaze, he moved toward the camera. "Who've you been looking at?"

His disregard of her clear invitation caught her off balance. "Wait."

Before she could stop him, he had the camera off the tripod and had begun to scroll through the photos. His brows lifted to find several of him from the last couple of days. Then there were a few of Manetto.

From tonight, there were at least five of Shelby. Ramos was with her in most of the shots, but there were a couple of close-ups of her. In the last, his hand rested on Shelby's back as he ushered her inside the club.

"So, who's the blond?" Sloan asked, peering at the camera from behind him.

Ramos glanced over his shoulder. "Why? You jealous?"

"No, of course not." His grin seemed to flame her temper even more, and she shook her head, then grabbed her empty coffee mug and hurried into the kitchen.

He placed the camera back on the tripod and followed her. "What time should I come by tomorrow?"

"You'd better come early, at least by eight. We have a lot of ground to cover."

She turned to face him, and he stepped close, invading her space. She backed up until she hit the kitchen counter and there was nowhere left to go. Her breath came fast, and their gazes met. Ramos wanted to kiss her in the worst way, but he hated being manipulated.

"I'm not playing this game with you," he said.

"Why not?" she murmured. "It was pretty fun last time."

That brought a smile to his lips, and he shook his head. "Maybe later...after the job." He stepped away and caught the flare of disappointment in her eyes. "I'm hoping that will be an extra incentive for you to make sure your team doesn't get trigger happy, and I come out if this alive."

She huffed out a disgruntled breath, and he stepped to the door.

"See you tomorrow." After shutting the door behind him, he hurried down the stairs. That was a narrow escape, and he didn't know if he felt relief or disappointment. Maybe a little of both.

Chapter 2

The next morning, Ramos arrived at Sloan's apartment early. He hadn't slept well, and this whole deal left him unsettled. He liked being the one in charge, and trusting her wasn't easy to do. So why didn't he tell her no?

Manetto had given him every opportunity to back out, but he hadn't, and now he hoped he didn't regret it. That's why he'd spent half the night coming up with a few plans of his own that he was willing to implement, with or without Sloan's knowledge.

"You're early," Sloan said, opening the door. "I'm not quite ready. Go ahead and get yourself some coffee."

She went back into her bedroom and shut the door. Instead of getting coffee, Ramos took the opportunity to glance around the room. Some papers lying on the floor next to the couch caught his eye, and he quickly picked them up.

Shock rippled through him to see his name in a police case file from Orlando. Only instead of Alejandro Ramos, it was his real name – Alejandro Ramirez.

The bedroom door opened, and he turned to face Sloan, his eyes tight with accusation. As she realized what he held in his hands, her face paled. "I can explain."

Ramos took a deep breath and clenched his jaw against the bitter anger that surged through his chest. He'd worked so hard to leave all of that behind him. Not even Manetto knew his real name. She might think she could hold this over his head, but he had friends of his own, and he wouldn't let it happen.

"You can't touch me with this," he said.

"That's not - I didn't do it for that reason."

"I find that hard to believe."

"Of course you would." She glanced at the papers, but instead of trying to snatch them back, her fierce gaze caught his. "Keep them if you want. I haven't told anyone your real identity, and I'm not going to."

Ramos narrowed his eyes, then folded the papers and stuffed them into the inner pocket of his jacket. He knew giving them to him was a futile attempt to appease him, since she probably had a lot of material on him stored somewhere. But it didn't matter. Alejandro Ramirez didn't exist anymore. So what did she plan to do with this information?

"I can't be bought," he said. "So whatever you had in mind, you should just forget it."

She shook her head and closed her eyes before facing him. "That was never my intent. And since you're being so close-minded about it, I don't think I'll ever tell you why I found it." She slipped on a black coat and pulled on some leather gloves. "Let's go."

Ramos followed her down the stairs and outside. Her car was parked behind the building, and she moved to open the door.

"Since I know where we're going, let's take my car," Ramos said. With a shrug, she followed him to the street where his black sports car was parked at the curb. They drove for a time without speaking, then Ramos broke the silence. "How many people are on your team?"

"There's five of us, if you count Antonio, who's working undercover with Carlos." She sent a quick glance his way. "Uh...just so you know...I had to tell them about you. To be honest, they're not too happy to be working with a mob-boss and his hit-man. But I got the okay from my superiors, so they can't touch you."

Ramos raised his brows, not reassured in the least. Did she really believe that? If they knew who he was, he'd be lucky to come out of this alive. Hell, if the bullets started flying, he'd probably be the first person they'd target. "Good to know."

He got on the freeway and drove to the industrial side of town, closer to the airport and some old abandoned buildings. Taking the exit, he drove several more blocks until coming to a set of dilapidated buildings at the end of a long entryway.

The largest building sported a few loading docks outside the warehouse, with all kinds of old drums and barrels left to rust. From what Ramos knew, this was an old paint factory. He wouldn't be surprised if some of the containers held toxic materials.

A smaller building to the side had been used as an office. The door had been broken down, and all the glass windows had been shattered by rock-throwing vandals. In such a sorry state, no one came out here, so it was a perfect place to do business.

"I think this might work," Sloan said, obviously impressed. She stepped inside the warehouse to take a look around, then did the same with the smaller office building.

"How do you want to do this?" Ramos asked.

"There's plenty of room inside to store the weapons. Carlos could get a good look at what we had and then, after he paid up, we could arrest him."

"You make it sound easy." Ramos shook his head. "Believe me, nothing is ever that easy."

"Well," she said, huffing out a disgruntled breath. "Do you have a better plan?"

"How about this," he began. "Your people are bringing them in a truck, right?" At her nod, he continued. "Then we park the truck there." He pointed to a space out in the open. "And take a few of the crates out of the back for him to inspect. After he looks through them, and he's satisfied that I'm not trying to cheat him, he pays me, and then you arrest him."

"I see how it is," she said, narrowing her eyes. "You're after the money."

"Hey, I've got to have some compensation for the risk I'm taking. I also have a reputation. I wouldn't want it getting out that I helped the feds."

As she thought it over, he continued, "There's plenty of places your men can hide. You could even put a couple of snipers on the roof if you wanted. With Carlos and his men out in the open, it's a nice set-up."

Sloan glanced around the area again, then turned to give him a grudging nod. "All right. It should work. Let's do it."

On the drive back to her apartment, Sloan explained that the truck with the weapons and the rest of her team were at the local army base about an hour out of town.

"They can have the truck with all the weapons here by tomorrow afternoon, so we can do this pretty quickly. First, we need to set up a meeting between you and Carlos. If that goes well, then you arrange the deal with him for tomorrow afternoon. With any luck, this whole thing could be over and done in time for Christmas."

Ramos nodded and shot her a quick glance. "You got someone to get home to?"

She shrugged. "My parents are always pretty happy to see me. Last year I was on an assignment and didn't make it, so...yeah, it would be nice. What about you?"

Ramos let out a breath. He didn't have a family to speak of, but he had plenty of friends in the Latin community who were always inviting him to their homes for carne asadas and pupusas. Most of them knew his reputation, and he'd ended up taking care of a few problems for them, so they were close in some ways, but not like a real family.

"I have plans."

"Anyone special?" she asked.

He chuckled. "My job is not exactly favorable to any type of a relationship, not that I don't have plenty of offers."

She shook her head. "I don't doubt that."

He smiled at her jealous tone. She obviously didn't like how easy he had it with women, and it warmed his heart. "If we're still alive once this is over, we might want to celebrate before you go home."

Her face broke into a cautious smile, but she wasn't about to give in so easily. "Hmm. How about this...if this deal goes through, I might even give you a Christmas present."

"Me?" he asked, feigning surprise. "Well...how can I pass that up?" She smiled like she had something up her sleeve, and he would have given anything to know what she was thinking.

He pulled to a stop in front of her building and turned to face her. "So what now?"

"I'm meeting with Antonio, my inside man, at noon. I'll tell him you're ready to make the deal and to have Carlos come to your club at ten tonight."

"Are you sure meeting with him is wise? What if someone sees you?"

"I'll take extra precautions, but I have to make sure no one can hear our conversation, which means we need to meet in person."

Ramos shook his head. This was all happening so fast. She'd just barely asked him to help out yesterday, but it was obvious this operation had been going on for some time. "How long have you been planning this whole thing?"

She ducked her head. "Not long."

"And you expect me to believe that?"

"Look...an opportunity presented itself, and I had to jump on it...that's the way things work in this business."

"Sure," he said, shrugging. "Then I guess I need a list of everything on that truck...before tonight."

"I've got the list right here." She pulled a manila folder from her bag and opened it up. "There's enough to start at five million, but I'm sure you'll have to come down from there."

He glanced through the papers, roughly estimating the cost and coming up with about the same amount. "That sounds about right. But Sloan...it all has to be there, or Carlos will shoot first and ask questions later."

"Trust me. It will be there."

Since he couldn't inspect the truck ahead of time, he'd have to take her word for it, but it bothered him more than he let on. "I guess you're coming to the club tonight, too?"

She shrugged. "I thought I would."

He let out a breath and glanced at her. "Is there anything else I need to know?"

"No," she said, but her gaze dropped to her lap, and Ramos tensed.

She glanced back at him, and he raised his brows, willing her to tell him more, but she pressed her lips together and moved to open the door. Before she could get out, he reached across her and pulled the door shut. "I get the feeling there's something else you're not telling me."

Mere inches from her face, his gaze traveled from her eyes to rest on her mouth. She licked her lips, and his resolve to keep his distance shattered. As he leaned in to kiss her, a satisfied smile creased her lips. Like a dash of cold water, it brought him to his senses, and he pulled back.

"Wait," Sloan said, her dark eyes filling with disappointment. "Look...I'm not at liberty to tell you everything, but you know enough to make this work. I know this is a big risk on your part, and I want you to know how much I appreciate it. I mean it. This deal wouldn't get off the ground without you."

He shook his head and sighed, unable to hold back his frustration. "You know...all day I've been asking myself why I was doing this. There's no logical explanation because, if you think about it, it's pretty stupid. You know who I am and what I do. You could be setting me up, for all I know. So why did I say I'd help you?"

She shrugged and let out a breath. "Maybe it's for old time's sake. We made a good team, even if you didn't know who I worked for."

"That's true. But I should have known better. I mean...you could out-shoot most of the hired thugs, and you even landed me on my butt a few times. But you're forgetting that we were in Mexico. You couldn't touch me there, so it didn't matter as much. This is different. You could haul me off to prison, and there would be nothing I could do about it."

"That's not going to happen."

"Tell that to your team."

"Ramos. I'll make sure nothing like that ever happens to you."

She almost made him believe that she meant it, and maybe she did, but it wasn't enough. It was up to him to make sure he survived, even if it meant deceiving her. "I hope that's good enough."

Her eyes widened in dismay, and she frowned. With a quick jerk on the handle, she opened the door. "I'll call you."

Ramos watched her disappear around the building. What a mess. He started the car and began the drive to Thrasher Development. It was too late to back out now, but it wasn't too late to make plans of his own and make sure he was ready for anything. He wished he could ask Shelby for her help on this, but putting her in danger was not an option. It was just something he'd have to manage on his own.

He pulled into the parking garage and soon joined Manetto in his office.

"How did it go?" Manetto asked.

"I think it will work." Ramos explained the plan, including the place for the exchange. "Sloan agreed to the exchange at the factory, so at least that part went right. Now I'm supposed to meet with Carlos at the club tonight and set it up for tomorrow."

"You sound upset. Is there something else going on?"

Ramos sighed. "I think there's something Sloan's not telling me...so yeah...I'm not happy about that. She is going along with the money transfer to our accounts, so at least that's good. Now if I just had Shelby's abilities, I'd feel a lot better about this."

Someone cleared her throat, and they turned to find Shelby standing beside the open door, her brow puckered with suspicion. "What's this about wanting my abilities?"

Ramos swore in his mind. From Shelby's raised brows, he was pretty sure she'd picked it up. He also realized that he hadn't blocked his thoughts about the deal and cursed again.

"Hmm...I'm not sure I like where this is going. What have you gotten yourself into?" Shelby asked him. Then she turned to Manetto. "He's thinking he might get killed."

"It's not as bad as it looks," Manetto said.

She glanced between them with disbelief and shook her head. "Selling weapons to a Mexican gun dealer? Wait...you're doing it for...a government agent? Are you serious?"

"How come you're here?" Manetto said, trying to take control of the situation.

"You asked me to come, remember? To talk to Jackie about a Christmas present."

"Oh, right."

"By the way...she doesn't want diamonds." Shelby glanced down the hall toward Jackie's desk, then closed the door behind her. "She was thinking about going on a trip. Did you know she's always wanted to go to Italy?"

"No," Manetto said, his eyes widening with alarm.

"Yeah. She wants to meet some of your relatives there and do the whole 'Find Yourself in Tuscany' thing."

"Well damn, I'll have to think about that."

"Right," Shelby answered, trying not to smile. "But if you want to get her diamonds...I think she'd like a necklace best."

"Okay...good to know."

"So what's going on?" She glanced pointedly at Ramos.

Before he could reply, Manetto turned to him. "You have to admit, having Shelby there tonight could be just what you need."

Ramos wasn't so sure about that. Usually when Shelby was involved, things tended to get a little crazy. What if it made things worse?

"I heard that," she said, raising her brow.

He huffed out a breath. "I didn't want to involve you in this, but...maybe if you could listen in, I'd get a better picture of what I'm up against." He quickly explained the whole story and hoped Shelby didn't pick up anything personal between him and Sloan.

"So this was her idea," Shelby said, shaking her head. "It doesn't take a mind-reader to know that you don't trust her...although I did pick up on that. Sheesh! She could be setting you up. Are you sure that's not what this whole thing is about?"

"No I'm not, but she said she's been after Carlos for a long time, so I think that's her main focus." He didn't add that she might have wanted to see him again...for old time's sake, then he did a mental head slap, knowing Shelby probably heard that.

"So she's after both you and Carlos, but for different reasons..." Shelby raised her brow in a way that always made him feel like he'd been caught doing something wrong. It irritated the hell out of him.

"But you don't trust her, so you're not sure. I can certainly see why you'd need me. Uh-oh..." Shelby let out a breath, apparently picking up more. "She told her team that you're a hitman for the mob? Holy hell! That's like putting a target on your back." She shook her head with astonishment. "Sheesh, and here I thought I was a trouble magnet."

"Dammit," Ramos said, not liking that she'd caught all of that from his mind before he'd had a chance to put up his barriers.

"Oh...um." She shrugged an apology. "I guess I wasn't supposed to hear that."

"No you weren't," he agreed.

She twisted her lips and met his gaze. "Maybe I wasn't. But, since I did, I just have to say that I don't like what's going on here. This has put you in a very bad place, and I think you really need me. Isn't there something I can do to help?"

Ramos couldn't be too mad at her for worrying about him, but he couldn't help wondering if it was because Sloan was an agent, or because she was an old lover. Then he caught Shelby's flushed face and hid a smile that she'd picked up on that.

In the silence, Manetto chimed in. "Why don't you come to the club tonight Shelby. Ramos is meeting with the gun dealer at ten, so I can have Ricky pick you up around nine."

"You'll need to come in the back way," Ramos added. "Because I'm pretty sure Sloan will be here in the club and probably watching the door. I'd rather she didn't know you were here."

"How would she know about me? Wait a minute...has she been spying on the club? Has she seen me?"

"Yes. But she doesn't know who you are, and I'm planning on keeping it that way. We can't afford to have another federal agent poking into your connection to us. It's bad enough that Blake thinks you have premonitions."

"Uh...okay." Her face went a little pale, and Ramos could see that the ramifications of the situation had finally dawned on her. He shook his head, hardly believing that she'd called him a trouble magnet when getting involved in stuff like this was her own fault.

Shelby caught his gaze, and he knew she'd picked that up. With her lips pressed together in annoyance, she straightened her shoulders and lifted her chin. "I'll be ready at nine."

"Thank you Shelby," Manetto chimed in. "We'll figure out the logistics tonight, once you get to the club."

"Okay. I'll see you then." She glanced between Ramos and Manetto, and it was easy to pick up that she was a little disgruntled by both of them. With a quick goodbye, she exited the room.

Manetto made sure the door was closed before turning to Ramos. "So how does Sloan know about Shelby?"

"She's staying in the apartment above the diner across the street. She's been taking photos of our comings and goings, and had one of Shelby from last night. She wanted to know who Shelby was, but I didn't tell her."

"Hmm...that's good to know. I guess I'll have to buy that building so something like this doesn't happen again."

Ramos shook his head, unsure that would prevent anyone from spying on them if they wanted to bad enough. "Sloan wants me to start at five million and go down from there. I think she's right, but will you take a look at this list?"

After studying the list, Manetto nodded his agreement. "Those rocket launchers go for thirty-two grand each, but on the black market we could easily get twice that much. The stinger missiles make up for the rest. Wow, this is quite the set-up. Where did she get all of these weapons?"

"Her boss."

"They must really want this guy." Manetto handed the sheet back to Ramos and rubbed his chin. "Are you sure there's no connection to the cartel in Mexico?"

"She showed me a picture of the dealer, Carlos. I've never seen him before, but she was just as involved as we were. I'd think if there was a connection, she would have told me."

Manetto nodded. "True, but it's a good thing Shelby will be there tonight. Is there any chance you can pull out? Sloan's not threatening you with anything, is she?"

"No. At least not yet. But who knows? Maybe she's saving it in case I try to back out."

Manetto sighed, clearly unhappy with the whole thing. "I'm almost sorry you're involved with this. But with Shelby's help, we'll figure it out. Just make sure that Shelby keeps her distance from Sloan. We wouldn't want her striking up a conversation with the agent."

Ramos chuckled. "You're right. She'd probably do it too, since that's the only way she'd really get Sloan thinking about me and her intentions. I'll have to tell her that she can't do that. But since we both know that Shelby doesn't always do what we tell her, I hope she'll listen this time."

Usually people did what Ramos told them, but not Shelby. She knew he had a soft spot in his heart for her, so it didn't work as well.

"I hope so too," Manetto agreed. "You also need to find out if Carlos has the money, so be sure to ask about that. Now let's set up the account for the money transfer today, so at least that will be ready."

Once everything was set up, Ramos left to get ready for the meeting, hoping that if he left nothing to chance, he might just make it out of this a free man.

Chapter 3

At eight o'clock, Ramos strode into the club and straight to the meeting room. He needed to make sure everything was ready, as well as find a place for Shelby to hide where she wouldn't be visible. That proved harder than he'd thought, since it was a big, open space without a closet in sight.

The room held a round, wooden table and upholstered chairs in the center, with a black leather couch along the wall and two stuffed chairs at the back. A beautiful, hardwood wet bar was nestled on the other side, complete with stools in front of the curved, granite-topped bar.

On the wall behind the bar was a sink with a matching granite countertop. Tall cupboards with tinted glass doors stood on both sides of the sink, and were filled with expensive varieties of liquor. A big-screen TV rested in the dark elegance of the upper middle cupboard.

He moved behind the wet bar and glanced inside the cabinets under the granite countertop. He found glasses stored there, along with some cleaning supplies. If he shifted them to the far side of the cabinet, there might be enough room for Shelby to squeeze inside.

After he moved everything over, his burner phone buzzed, and he fished it out of his pocket. "Yes."

"Everything's set up," Sloan said. "Carlos will be there at ten."

"Do you know how many men he's bringing with him?"

"Probably two," she answered.

"Is your guy one of them?"

"I don't think so. He's not high enough in the ranks. If the deal falls through, he's the first person they'd want to kill since he set it up. So we'll just have to make sure that doesn't happen."

"Okay," Ramos said. "I'll be taking Carlos into a private room to talk. Once we're done, I'll come out and find you."

"Shouldn't I come to the meeting?"

"No." Ramos braced for her argument, but heard only silence before she finally answered.

"Fine. But don't make me regret this."

He took a breath, but refrained from telling her that he already regretted this whole deal. "Don't worry, Sloan. You'll get what you came for." Satisfied with his comeback, he disconnected before she could answer.

Since Ricky had left to get Shelby, he called the two men who worked as bouncers to the room and informed them about the meeting with the arms dealer, making sure they were prepared for Carlos's visit.

"He'll have two men with him. I want you to pat all of them down outside before you let them into the club. If they have weapons, tell them to come back without them. Once you've cleared them, I'll want Ricky to escort them to this room while you wait outside this door."

He sent them back to their posts and checked the room one more time, but couldn't come up with a better place for Shelby. It might be a little cramped, but there wasn't another option, and he hoped she'd be okay with it.

Devil in a Black Suit 33

A knock sounded at the door, and Shelby stepped inside. He took one look at her and smiled. She had on her black wig and the black clothes he'd purchased for her a while back.

"Going incognito?" he asked.

"Well, you said the agent had pictures of me," she replied. "So I thought it might be best." She looked him over with an appreciative nod. "Hmmm...You've sure got the whole crime boss thing going in that black suit. I think Carlos will be impressed."

Just to get a rise out of her, he tilted his lips into a sexy grin and thought that Carlos wasn't the only person he wanted to impress.

"You dressed up for Sloan, too?" Shelby asked.

Ramos chuckled since she'd missed that he'd wanted to impress her as well. "Hey. I have a reputation to uphold, and I need to dress the part. It impressed you, didn't it?"

"Well...yeah." Her gaze caught his and she swallowed, clearly captivated by his good looks and trying not to be. "You're like a devil in a black suit."

His grin widened, and he nodded. "I like that."

"Try not to let it go to your head." She glanced around the room, and her brows drew together. "There's no place in here for me to hide."

"Yes there is," Ramos said. "There's a spot back here." He motioned to the other side of the bar, and she followed him behind it.

"On the floor?"

"No." Ramos held back a smile, then opened the cupboard door inside the bar. "In there. I've already moved out all the stuff that was in there, so you should have plenty of room."

Shelby's gaze flew to his. "You can't be serious? That's way too small."

"But...you're small enough to fit, aren't you?" His gaze traveled leisurely over her body, and he held back a smile as her face turned pink. Then he looked inside the cupboard. "Hmm...it might be tight, but it should work."

He glanced around the room, pretty sure there wasn't another option. But she could probably sit back here on the floor and it would be all right, as long as Carlos stayed on the other side of the bar.

"Wait...you're serious?" Shelby let out a breath. "Fine, I'll try it. But it looks pretty cramped in there. I might not last long."

"I promise to keep the meeting short. After he leaves, we'll head out into the club. I've got someone watching for Sloan, so I'll have you slip out first and get as close to where she is as possible. But don't talk to her."

Shelby caught his gaze, and her eyes widened. She frowned and shook her head, clearly upset. "You think I'll say something to her, don't you? And ruin everything. I'm not going to do that."

"Good. I'll try and ask her leading questions so you can get everything you need."

She nodded, but didn't say anything, and he knew he'd hurt her feelings. "Once she leaves, we'll come back in here, and you can tell me what you found out."

"Sure," she agreed, but it didn't take a rocket scientist to know she wasn't real happy with him.

"You know that I appreciate your help, Shelby," he said, hoping to smooth things over. "I wouldn't ask this of you if it wasn't important."

"I know, I know," she said. "I owe you, so don't worry about it."

He hoped that wasn't the only reason she helped him, but even if it was, he was more than grateful. He wouldn't involve her at all if he thought it would put her in danger.

Still, he wished he could tell her he was sorry he'd hurt her feelings...but he just couldn't make the words come out of his mouth. Bad guys like him didn't apologize...for anything.

Shelby huffed out a breath and shook her head, clearly picking up his thoughts. "Fine. I forgive you."

Ramos smiled, happy he'd apologized without saying a word. Maybe having her hear his thoughts wasn't so bad. Before she could respond, a knock sounded at the door, and Ramos checked his watch. "He's early. Let me make sure it's him before you get in."

He left her at the bar and hurried to open the door. Ricky stood there with Carlos and two men waiting behind him. "Someone here to see the boss," Ricky said.

Ramos knew it would give him away to look at Shelby, so he told her in his thoughts to get inside the cupboard. Deliberately taking his time, he looked over the men, then directed his attention back to Ricky, and opened the door wide enough to allow them inside. "Bring them in."

Ricky stepped back to let Carlos and his men into the room, then followed them in. "You must be Carlos," Ramos began. "I'm Ramos. Manetto asked me to handle this deal."

Carlos narrowed his eyes, then gave Ramos a quick nod. "As long as you have the merchandise, I'm fine working with you."

"Good. Come in and let's get acquainted." He motioned to the table, then nodded at Ricky who took up a position behind Ramos and facing Carlos's two men. They took the hint, and both moved back to stand in front of the door.

"Would you like something to drink?" Ramos asked. At Carlos's affirmative answer, he moved behind the bar, finding Shelby scrunched inside the cupboard with the door wide open, and her lips pursed with exasperation. Hiding his smile, he gently pushed the door closed, but left it opened a crack so she could hear their conversation. Then he picked up a bottle, and poured a shot of expensive whiskey into two glasses.

He took them to the table. After handing one to Carlos, he sat down. Taking his time, he took a swallow, and leaned back in his chair. "I just have a few questions before we get started. As a precaution, I'd like to know who referred you to Manetto."

Carlos's brows rose with surprise. "One of my men has been asking around. He got the information from one of your people."

"Do you have a name?" Ramos pressed.

Carlos fidgeted in his seat before giving up his intel. "It was a woman. We've seen him meet with her a few times, but we don't have her name."

"Describe her."

"Long, dark hair, skin like yours, dark eyes...a real bonita."

Ramos nodded. So they'd spotted Sloan. That was good to know. "Yes...that's her." Ramos studied him for a long minute, hoping to keep him off balance. "All right. Let's get down to business." He opened the folder he'd previously placed on the table and handed the papers to Carlos. "Here's a list of everything that we have for sale."

Carlos took them and studied the contents while Ramos kept a watchful eye on him and his men. After a moment, Carlos put the papers down. "This is just what I am looking for. What is your price?"

"Five million."

"That seems a little steep."

"Is it too much for you?"

"No," Carlos said.

Ramos raised a brow. "It's a damn good price when you consider that everything on that list has never been used before."

Carlos glanced back at the paper, and Ramos wished Shelby could tell him what he was thinking. Too bad she was stuffed in the cupboard.

"I need to see them before I decide," Carlos said.

Ramos narrowed his gaze. "Are you questioning my reputation?"

Carlos pressed his lips together, realizing his mistake. "Not at all. But I still want to see them."

"You can see them when we make the exchange and not before. Take it or leave it."

Carlos took a deep breath, then nodded. "You have a deal."

"Good. As far as payment goes, I have an account set up for an electronic transfer."

"That will work. Will the exchange be here?"

Ramos smiled. "No. I'll text you with the location tomorrow, around four in the afternoon. All I need is your cell phone number."

Carlos's lips twisted, and he gave Ramos a hard stare, but Ramos just stared back. After letting out his breath a few times, Carlos finally nodded and gave Ramos his number. After entering the number, Ramos sent Carlos a text to make sure he had it right.

"Everything will be on a truck and ready for you to pick up tomorrow," Ramos said.

"I'm counting on it," Carlos said. "And should this deal fall through for some reason, it will not go well for you or your boss."

Ramos leaned back in his chair with raised brows. "Carlos, I'm surprised that you would threaten me. If anything, I'm the one taking the risk here. You know my reputation, but what do I know of yours?"

Carlos held perfectly still before sending Ramos a reluctant nod. "You will get your money, and I will get my weapons. We will both leave happy."

Ramos held his gaze for a second longer than he needed to. Then he nodded and stood. "Then I guess we're done here."

Carlos stood as well. After a quick nod to Ramos, he motioned to his men. Ricky opened the door and escorted them out, shutting it softly behind him.

"That was interesting," Ramos said, coming around the bar to help Shelby out of the cupboard. "I get the feeling that he doesn't like me much."

"You don't know the half of it," Shelby said, taking his hand and letting him help her stand. This close to him, he noticed her take a whiff of his cologne before she stepped away. Letting out a small sigh that he was sure he wasn't supposed to hear, she straightened her back and stretched. "I'm never sitting in a cupboard again."

Ramos grinned, pretty sure her moan included more than her aching back. "I'm sure Manetto would be happy to build a better hiding spot for you. I'll let him know."

Shelby opened her mouth to respond, but a knock sounded at the door. Her startled gaze flew to his.

"I don't know who that is," he responded. "But if it's Sloan, you might have to get back in the cupboard."

Another knock came, and Shelby let out an exasperated breath before scrunching down and scooting back into the small space. After she pulled her legs inside, Ramos left the cupboard door ajar and hurried to the door. He pulled it open, finding Sloan with a frown on her face. Even with the frown, she looked gorgeous in a short, black dress with tall heels, and her hair twisted artfully on top of her head. A crooked grin spread across his lips. Had she dressed up for him?

"If I didn't know better, I'd think somebody else was in here," she said, glancing inside the room.

Ramos raised his brows, and she took that moment to push her way inside. "Nice," she said, her gaze taking in the opulent furnishings, then she turned back to look him over. "You too. You look good in a black suit." With a sly smile, she motioned to the room. "So is this where Manetto makes all of his deals?"

Not waiting for an answer, she walked over to the bar. Ramos held his breath as she ran her fingers over the granite counter-top. As she turned to face him, he let it out. Just then the door opened and Ricky stuck his head inside. His eyes widened in surprise to find Sloan there. "Uh...they're gone."

"Thank you." Ramos turned to Sloan and motioned to the chair at the table. "Why don't you sit down, and I'll tell you what happened." He glanced at Ricky, who stood uncertainly in the doorway. "That will be all for now."

Ricky nodded and closed the door. After Sloan sat down, Ramos relaxed. "What can I get you to drink?"

"I'll have what you're having," she said.

Coming around the counter, he glanced through the crack in the cupboard door and caught a glimpse of Shelby's pained expression. He knew he'd be in trouble if he didn't figure out a way to get Sloan to leave as soon as possible. After pouring Sloan a drink, he stepped back to the table and handed her the glass before sitting down.

"Thanks," she said, taking a sip. "So how did it go?"

"It looks like we have a deal." He told her everything, including Carlos's veiled threat. "I don't trust him. But other than that, he's agreed to my terms."

She nodded. "Good. We can work with that."

"Did you know they made you?" he asked.

Her brows rose in surprise. "What do you mean?"

"I asked Carlos where his referral came from, and he said one of his men met with a woman whose description sounds just like you. It looks like they've been keeping tabs on your inside man, and now Carlos thinks you're one of my people." Ramos shook his head. "I'd sure hate for this to blow up in our faces. Do you think your guy would talk if they tortured him?"

Sloan's brow puckered. "That's not going to happen. I can only think of one time when they could have spotted us talking, and I made sure I wasn't followed when I left, so they don't have anything else on me."

"I hope you're right." From what he'd picked up from Carlos, he didn't seem sophisticated enough to know if he was being set up. But Ramos wasn't about to take Sloan's word for it, and he decided to change his plans to include a scenario where Carlos knew all about Sloan. That reminded him of Shelby. She would know, and it relieved him to have her help.

"So what's the plan for tomorrow?" he asked.

Sloan tipped her glass back and drank the rest of it all at once. She caught Ramos staring at her and smiled. "I think this is cause for celebration. Why don't you come back to the apartment, and we'll work it all out there?"

A tiny squeaking sound came from the cupboard, and Ramos cleared his throat before giving Sloan his sexiest grin, hoping to distract her in case she'd heard it.

"Uh...you're killing me here, but...I can't," he said, hoping to sound regretful. "Maybe once this is over..."

"Sure...I get it," Sloan said, glancing around the room, like she was trying to figure out where the noise had come from. After a moment, she shook her head and caught his gaze. "I can have the truck there by three-thirty. I know you'll want to check everything out before you make the call to Carlos. Why don't you come to the old factory then?"

Ramos nodded, sensing that she didn't want him there any earlier, and it made him suspicious. Did she have other plans that she didn't want him to know about? "Okay. One more thing...will your team be out of sight, or were you planning to pass them off as my men?"

Sloan held his gaze and shrugged. "Actually, now that Carlos thinks I'm one of your people, I can be by your side the whole time."

"I wouldn't object to that," he agreed. "What about the others?"

She glanced away. "I think we need a couple to pose as your men. I might have the others somewhere else, but it's something we can figure out when we get there."

He frowned, and she placed her hand on his arm. "Ramos, you don't have to worry. I'll be there, and I'll watch your back. Once Carlos transfers you the money, you could even get in your car and leave before I signal my team to move in."

Did she really think he'd agree to that? Even if he left, that didn't mean someone from her team wouldn't take a shot at him. "That's a nice idea. But I think I'll stick with you if that's all right." Ramos refrained from telling her about his own plans. He'd tell her tomorrow if he needed to, even if she wouldn't like it.

She nodded with obvious relief. "Good." She held his gaze for a moment, like she wanted him to change his mind about going back to her place, but he refrained from giving her any kind of encouragement.

She let out a breath and stood. "I guess that's it, then. Call me on the burner phone if you have any questions."

He sent her a nod.

She caught his gaze one last time and raised her brow, lifting her lips in a seductive smile. "You sure you don't want to come home with me?"

He smiled back, but shook his head with a low groan, and closed his eyes against the temptation.

"Okay. We'll finish this later." She sauntered to the door and, with one last seductive glance over her shoulder, she left.

Ramos took a deep breath and let it out. Then he jumped up and hurried over to the cupboard, hoping that Shelby wasn't too upset with him. "Sorry about that." He leaned down and offered her his hand. She grabbed it and slowly inched out of the cupboard, then staggered to her feet. Groaning, she stretched out her back and let out a breath.

"Can I get you something?" Ramos asked.

Shelby shook her head and refused to look him in the eyes, clearly embarrassed. Ramos hid a smile and opened the small refrigerator. He pulled out a bottle of water and handed it to her. As she took it, her wide-eyed gaze caught his, and he frowned. "What?"

"She's...she's got ulterior motives."

If Ramos wasn't mistaken, he'd think she was jealous. "Like what?" Shelby blushed, and he couldn't help smiling. "You mean...like making wild love with me?"

"Well...yes...that was obvious."

He grinned at her discomfort. "Come sit down on the couch where it's comfortable." He glanced at the couch and imagined sitting there with Shelby's soft body nestled against his.

With a groan, Shelby quickly slipped into a chair at the table.

"Or not...why don't we start with Carlos and go from there."

Ramos sat in his chair, but slid it next to hers, noticing as he did that she didn't move away. Maybe she wasn't too mad at him. He hid a smile and bent his head toward hers. "So, what's up with Carlos?"

She blew out a breath and sat up straight in her chair. "Uh...Carlos may have come for the weapons, but it wasn't hard to lure him here." Shelby shook her head and let out a sigh. "There's so much going on with that guy that I wish I could have taken notes." She caught Ramos's gaze. "But none of it's good."

"What does that mean?" Ramos could hardly believe he had to worry about Carlos. Maybe Shelby was being overly dramatic?

"I'm not being overly dramatic." She pursed her lips in frustration. "In fact, I'm pretty sure he wants to kill you."

Ramos's brows rose in surprise. "Oh...uh...I didn't see that coming. So what's going on?" Shelby seemed genuinely upset, so it had to be true. It also warmed his heart that she cared so much about him...more than she seemed willing to admit. He liked it...a lot.

She let out a dramatic sigh and closed her eyes. Ramos took that opportunity to lean in a little closer. She glared at him but didn't move away, and he took that as a good sign. Then she shook her head and got back to business.

"Uh...Carlos was thrilled that Uncle Joey wanted you to take over the deal, since you're the reason he wanted to do the deal in the first place. It seems like he's got something against you."

She caught his gaze and furrowed her brows. "What happened in Mexico? It seems like this is all tied up with that...I mean, you obviously met Sloan there...and now Carlos, too?"

Ramos frowned. "You know what happened. We had to take down that cartel to save Carlotta and Miguel."

"Well...yeah, I know. But Carlos is holding a grudge against you. Are you sure you've never met him before?"

"Yes. I'm positive."

"Okay...well, I couldn't get the whole story because it was just in bits and pieces. First off, I think there's something about Sloan that he doesn't like. But I couldn't pick up more than that."

"Maybe it's just that he thinks she's working for me," Ramos suggested.

"Maybe," Shelby agreed. "But I think you must have killed someone important to him. So I'm pretty sure he's hoping to kill you sometime during the deal, or after...whatever works best. And I think there's money involved, too, but that doesn't make sense." Shelby's lips turned down, and worry tightened her forehead.

"Hmm," Ramos said. "That surprises me. I know I've never met Carlos before, so I don't know why he'd want to kill me, but if that's what he was thinking...it must be true." He caught her gaze. "If you hadn't come tonight, I wouldn't have known. This changes things."

"So you're not going through with it?" she asked, her voice hopeful.

Ramos shook his head. "Knowing he's out to kill me isn't going to stop me from going ahead with the deal, but it will make all the difference in the outcome. I'm sure of that."

Shelby let out her breath, clearly unhappy with his decision. Then she glanced up at him with a gleam in her eyes. "Maybe I should come with you. I could warn you."

Ramos's brows rose. Was she out of her mind? Not only would he have to worry about getting killed himself, but he'd have to keep her from getting killed, too. "I don't think that's a good idea, but I appreciate the thought."

Her gaze dropped, and she shrugged like she didn't care, but he knew he'd hurt her feelings. Still...he didn't want her to get hurt, and he hoped she knew that.

"I know...it's okay." She caught his gaze and her lips tilted into that sweet smile that always caught at his heartstrings. "I understand. Besides, you've got a back-up plan, right?"

"Yeah," he agreed, careful not to think about his plan. "I'll be fine."

"Good."

"So...what did you pick up from Sloan?" Then he couldn't help adding, "Besides her ulterior motives to get me in the sack?"

Shelby rolled her eyes and shook her head. "Uh...she's honest about catching these guys, so that's good. But she's worried that Carlos might try something. I picked up that she's really gone out on a limb to catch him, so I think there might be more to it. It's almost like she's out for revenge for some reason. But maybe that's how she feels about all the bad guys." She caught Ramos's gaze. "Except for you, of course."

He grinned, and she shook her head, then leaned her shoulder next to his and kept her gaze on her bottle of water. "She's also worried about her team and how they might react toward you if something goes wrong."

Shelby pulled away and glanced up at him. "So, now it looks like you have to worry about both sides coming after you. This is terrible. It's like you're in this totally alone. You really should consider calling the deal off."

He hated dashing her hopes, but he wasn't about to do that. "You're forgetting something."

"What?"

"I'm used to people wanting me dead. That's the kind of life I lead...remember?" He'd never forget the day he'd met

Shelby, and he'd killed a man to save her life. She shouldn't either. "So what else did you get from Sloan?"

Shelby let out a disappointed sigh. "Uh...she seemed genuinely relieved that she could be by your side during the exchange, not just to watch her men, but to keep an eye on you, too. As far as the money goes, she doesn't have a problem with you getting it, as long as she doesn't lose the weapons."

"That's good."

"There's one more thing." Shelby glanced away and chewed on her bottom lip.

"What?"

She let out a breath and caught his gaze. "She's hiding something from you. I'm not sure what it is, but I think it's something that might be important to you personally. And it's...something from your past."

Ramos nodded. "I already knew that. I found some papers at her place with my former last name on them. And get this; they came from the Orlando police department. I'd like to know why she's looking into my background."

Shelby's eyes widened with surprise. "Yeah...no kidding. Do you think she's trying to find some dirt on you so she can set you up?"

He chuckled. "Babe. She wouldn't need to look into my background for dirt."

"Oh...right," she said. "Well, then I hope she's not trying to build a case to put you in prison or something."

"We have a deal," Ramos said, needing to come to Sloan's defense.

"Yeah...well...then I hope she sticks to it."

Ramos frowned at Shelby's skepticism, mostly because it mirrored his own. He knew he couldn't trust Sloan, even if he wanted to. Still, something about her begged him to try.

But was it worth the risk? Probably not. "I'll make sure she can't touch me...at least in that sense."

Shelby rolled her eyes, picking up his hint. "Yeah...whatever." She opened her mouth to say something, then just as quickly closed it.

"What?" Ramos asked.

"Nothing."

"There's something else you picked up from her. What is it?"

"I'm not sure I should tell you," she said.

"Is it about the deal?"

"No."

"Oh...so it's personal?" He grinned, picking up Shelby's discomfort. "After Mexico, I never thought I'd see her again. Did she miss me?"

"I'm not talking to you about that, so you'll just have to figure it out for yourself. Just make sure she doesn't double-cross you. And don't let Carlos kill you, either."

"I have a plan that neither of them will know about, so I'll be fine."

Shelby lifted her brow. "You can say that, but we both know you only sort of have a plan. That's not the same thing."

Ramos narrowed his gaze and held hers until she squirmed. He didn't need her telling him what to do. He had it under control. Sure, he had some loose ends to tie up, but now that he knew what Carlos intended, he'd work it out.

"Okay. Fine," Shelby said, picking up his thoughts. "Then I guess you don't need me anymore."

She stood to leave, and a stab of remorse rushed over him. "Shelby," he said, catching her arm and standing beside her. "Thanks for coming tonight. I mean it."

She kept her gaze averted, then slowly turned her face toward his. Their gazes met and something unfurled in Ramos's heart. He knew Shelby truly cared about him, without any strings attached. It filled him with warmth.

"Just...promise me you'll be careful," Shelby said.

"I will." Ramos's gaze drifted to her lips. This close, it would be so easy to lean down and kiss her.

With a small gasp, Shelby pulled away, breaking the spell. He shook his head and shrugged. Knowing she was probably listening to his thoughts, he tried to cover how much she rattled him by giving her a sexy grin. "Hey, give me a break. I might die tomorrow."

She shook her head at his attitude and kept backing up. "Uh...I'd better go." Her back foot caught the chair leg and knocked it sideways. She reached out to grab it and then shoved it toward the table between them. "Uh...good luck tomorrow." She grabbed her coat from the coatrack and pulled the door open.

Ricky straightened from his stance on the other side of the door and stepped inside the room. "Ready to go?"

"Yeah," she answered.

"You should go out the back way, in case anyone's watching," Ramos said.

"Okay," she agreed. "Bye." With one last glance at him, Shelby disappeared out the door.

Ramos blew out a breath, knowing he walked a fine line with her. As much as he liked teasing her, he didn't want to let his emotions get involved. She meant more to him than someone to toy with, so even though it bolstered his ego that he could get under her skin, it wasn't something he should take advantage of. She was a good person and deserved better.

From the beginning, Shelby had treated him differently. She always looked at him as a good person first, where most everyone else always saw the bad. At least for her, he wanted to be a better person. Because of that, he needed to treat her right and not step across the line.

But none of that applied to someone like Carlos. Ramos knew he wouldn't hesitate to kill Carlos if he had to. Now that he knew Carlos's true intentions, it was time to figure out a plan to make sure Carlos didn't get the chance to kill Ramos first.

Despite the late hour, he called an old friend, who was happy to sell him what he needed, and left the club to pick it up. For the first time that day, something settled inside him. With a grim smile, he even looked forward to the confrontation with Carlos. It might be tricky to put his plan into action, and he might not even need it if Sloan was true to her word, but it would still be there just in case.

Chapter 4

The sun was shining bright at three-thirty the next afternoon. But, with the temperature in the mid-thirties, it was cold enough to see his breath. Ramos parked his car about a block away from the paint factory and pulled out the burner phone. He wanted to make sure Sloan knew he was coming so none of her people would take a shot at him.

"It's me," he said. "I'm here. Is it safe to come in?"

"Yes, of course. We've been expecting you."

He disconnected and, with his lips pressed into a grim line, he turned down the street and onto the property. It had taken him most of the morning to gather everything he needed for his plan. He'd also taken extra precautions with his equipment, wearing his high-grade Kevlar vest under his black utility jacket. His cargo pants held all kinds of hidden compartments where he kept a small supply of knives, wire, and money.

But nothing compared to the guns he had strapped to his side and ankle, or the AK-47 in the trunk of his car, along with the crate that held his biggest surprise. He figured

Sloan would have a gun or two for him, but he wasn't about to leave his survival up to her.

He'd spent a small fortune on his black utility boots, which he'd had specially made a few years ago. They contained all kinds of places for sharp-edged knives, razors, and wires, things that no one would ever find. He'd learned from experience that it never hurt to be over-the-top when it came to being prepared, and today was one of those days.

Sloan stood in front of the big truck, and he pulled up beside her and stopped. She wore all black, with a warm jacket and a beanie hat pulled over her head. A rifle hung from her shoulder, and her smile reminded him of the first time he'd ever seen her.

She'd been dressed the same way then, only with her hair in a ponytail. That same fierce smile brought back all of his memories of working with her, and the torrid affair they'd had. Now, here they were again. Only this time was different, and he had to remember that.

He got out of the car, noting the four men and one woman that stood together around the truck. That was one more than she'd told him. They glanced his way with suspicion as well as curiosity, sizing him up.

Sloan came to his side and introduced him to her team, making sure to mention that, without him, none of this would be happening. They nodded, but didn't offer to shake hands or get too close. "We've unloaded a few of the crates and opened them for Carlos," she said.

At the back of the truck, Ramos looked them over, a little amazed that she had managed to get her hands on these military-grade weapons. "That's quite the arsenal. I can't believe your superiors let you take these." He caught her gaze. "If Carlos manages to get away with them..."

"That's not going to happen," she broke in, then glanced at her team. "We know the drill, and we're ready. We're not going to blow this chance to catch him."

Ramos raised his brow. He'd never understand why someone like Carlos had to be caught when killing him would do just as well. "So you're trying to make an example of him?"

"Yes. We're sending a message to the cartels."

Ramos nodded, glancing at her team for their reaction. Most of them seemed straight out of boot camp, but an older man with a shaved head held the hard gaze of someone who'd killed before. Ramos sent him a nod and got a small acknowledgement in return.

Satisfied, he glanced into the truck. Several crates were stacked on top of each other, and he knew that would never work. "I can guarantee you that Carlos will want to look through all of those crates. You'll have to take most of them out, and leave the rest uncovered so he can look inside of them. It will save time to do it now, and we can keep the weapons fairly close to the truck."

"All right," Sloan agreed. With the others, she got to work unloading the truck. Ramos took that opportunity to pop open his trunk and snag his rifle. He slung it over his shoulder and waited until no one was watching before unloading the small crate he'd brought. He discreetly set it on the ground beside the others.

His crate matched the others perfectly, although it was a little smaller. If anyone opened it, they'd find it filled with ammo for the M16's, and never give it a second thought.

Ramos got to work helping unload several more crates until they were all accessible. Then he turned to Sloan. "Have you got a tracker in there somewhere?"

Her eyes widened. "Uh...yeah, I do."

"Good. While you pry a few of the crates open, I'm going to move my car."

"You can park it by mine over there." She pointed to the other side of the office building.

After moving his car, he rejoined the rest of the team at the truck and checked his watch. "It's time to make the call. Are you ready?"

"I think so," Sloan said.

Ramos pulled out his cell phone and sent Carlos the text with the address. Carlos responded saying he was on his way. Sloan's team members dispersed to their positions, with one going to a spot on the warehouse roof, and another to hide behind some barrels closer to the truck. A third person hid inside the office building.

That left four of them beside the truck, all armed and dangerous. Ramos took the extra time to glance inside each of the crates, making sure all of the promised weapons were accounted for. He admired the rocket launchers, and pulled one of them out of the crate, hoisting it to his shoulder with ease.

"You ever fire one of these?" he asked the soldier standing beside him.

"Yes sir," the man said, his lips curving in a smile. "About knocked me off my feet."

Ramos chuckled, knowing that feeling well. He put the weapon back in the crate and faced the group. "I have it on good authority that Carlos might want me dead, which I'm afraid could include all of you, so I'd appreciate it if you'd keep your weapons handy."

None of them showed any surprise at his remark, and he glanced at Sloan. She came to his side and motioned him away from the others. "What makes you think that?" she asked.

"Just something he said last night. Did you ever meet him?"

"Me? No." She shook her head and glanced away, leaving Ramos suspicious that she was hiding something.

"What's going on?" he asked.

She opened her mouth to respond, but was interrupted by one of her men. "Here they come."

Ramos clenched his jaw in frustration, then took his position in front of the group and lowered his rifle. A black SUV, just like the ones favored by the feds, entered the property, and dread coursed down his spine. A moment of sheer panic that Sloan had set him up nearly overwhelmed him, then just as quickly retreated once the car came closer, and he could see Carlos sitting in the passenger side of the front seat.

Swearing in his mind, he couldn't ignore the irony that he was more relieved to see a Mexican gun dealer who wanted him dead than a federal agent.

The SUV pulled to a stop several feet away, and Carlos, along with four other men, got out of the car. They all had rifles slung across their shoulders and approached him warily. Ramos waited for them to get closer before he eased his finger off the trigger of his rifle.

"They're all here, just like I promised," Ramos said to him. "Go ahead and look them over." He turned to his team and motioned them back. "Give these guys some room."

After moving a respectful distance, Ramos watched Carlos, along with his second in command, inspect each crate. The other three men kept their gazes glued on Ramos and their rifles ready. It took several minutes before Carlos was satisfied, and the strain between the groups grew. It was enough to fill Ramos with foreboding, and he tensed under the pressure.

At last, Carlos and his men backed away. Ramos relaxed slightly, and moved toward Carlos to meet him halfway between their groups to finish the deal. "Are you satisfied?" Ramos asked.

"Yes. I believe it is all there. I just have one favor to ask. As you can see, we have no way to transport them. Would you be willing to include the truck in the transaction?"

"I think so," Ramos said. "For an extra fifty grand."

Carlos took a breath and frowned, then he gave Ramos a quick nod. "You drive a hard bargain, but I will add the money. The crates need to be reloaded. I hope you don't mind if I wait to pay you until the truck is ready to go."

Ramos couldn't find anything wrong with that, so he motioned to his team to get started and kept a close watch on Carlos and his men, nodding at Sloan to do the same.

After the truck was reloaded, and the back locked and secured, Carlos took out his phone. "Let me access my bank account, and then you can give me your account number."

Ramos took out his phone and, at Carlos's nod, repeated the numbers. Carlos asked for clarification on a couple of numbers. Ramos repeated them again, but unease washed over him. Was Carlos stalling?

Finally, Carlos told Ramos that he'd made the transfer and the money was on the way. Relieved, Ramos watched his screen for the transfer, but after more than a minute, it still hadn't come.

Suspicion washed over him, and he glanced at Carlos. In that unguarded moment, Ramos caught a gleam of triumph in Carlos's eyes, and he knew he'd been had. Just as Ramos brought his gun up to fire, Carlos lunged behind one of his men. The bullet hit the man in the chest, and Carlos got a shot off that caught Ramos in his ribs.

The force knocked him back, and he lost his grip on his rifle. Shooting broke out, and two of Carlos's men went down. Three more came out of the SUV to take their places, and Sloan yelled to take cover.

Huffing with pain, Ramos grabbed his rifle and staggered to a crouch, taking a couple of shots. Under fire, he rushed to take cover behind a group of barrels, grateful he'd worn his bullet-proof vest. He might have a couple of cracked ribs, but at least he wasn't dead.

Just then, the sound of a helicopter roared overhead. Dismayed, he glanced up to see a man with a machine gun hanging out of the door and targeting his guy on the roof.

Ramos took a couple of shots at the helicopter before coming under fire from Carlos's men. As he ducked behind the barrels, Sloan slid into a spot next to him, breathing heavily. They managed to get a few shots off, but heavy fire pinned them down.

"We have to move," Ramos said. "Run to the building and I'll cover you. On three...one, two, go!"

Sloan ran hard, and Ramos rose from his position to take a few shots at the men. After she made it safely to the building, she motioned him to run while she covered him. He took another shot, then ran to the building, sliding inside as shots rang around him.

The truck engine started up, and Ramos's heart sank. If they got too far away, they'd be out of range for his back-up plan to do any good. He ducked out to take a couple of shots, but machine gun fire from the chopper ripped into the ground in front of him, forcing him back. Helpless, he held his position, listening as the truck left the property.

The chopper stayed put for another minute, keeping them pinned down, then roared away. As soon as it was clear, Ramos ran from the building. One team member was down, and two others hurried to take stock of his injuries. He hated to think what had happened to the sniper on the roof, but at least the one in the office building had joined them unscathed.

Sloan took charge, directing someone to check on the sniper's condition, and pulled out her phone to call for an ambulance.

Ramos ran toward the road, hoping to catch sight of the truck, but it was nowhere to be seen. He knew there wasn't much time before they'd lose them, and he hurried back to Sloan. "I'm going after them."

"Wait. I'm coming with you." She shouted instructions to one of her men and caught up to him. They ran to his car and jumped inside.

As Ramos peeled out of the lot, Sloan pulled the tracker from her pocket. The chopper was long gone, but there was a chance they could catch up to the slow-moving truck.

"You have a signal?" Ramos asked.

"Yes. They're headed north."

Ramos turned in that direction and floored it. "There's not much out that way except the airport and a few other airstrips. I'll bet anything that's where they're headed."

They got to the main highway and turned east before heading north again. The road joined onto a bigger highway which would take them to the main airport.

"Okay. You need to stay to the left," Sloan instructed. "They've turned off the road to head west."

"Got it." Ramos took the next exit and followed the road. A few miles later, he spotted a hangar and a few small planes in the distance. "Is that where they are?"

"I think so. The truck must have just gotten there, because the signal's not moving anymore. What should we do? Is that a private airstrip?"

"It could be. I've never been out here before. See if you can spot a bigger plane. The ones I can see are too small to carry all the weapons."

"Maybe it hasn't landed yet," Sloan said.

"Don't count on it. This was too organized for them to be waiting on a plane." He turned toward the airstrip and caught sight of a bigger plane on the other side of the hangar. "There it is."

"I'm calling for back-up."

"It won't matter," Ramos said. "They'll be long gone before anyone ever gets here. We need to find a way in while they're busy loading."

"I'm still calling." Sloan took out her phone and made the call, while Ramos turned toward the airstrip. A group of office buildings and a car rental stood several yards behind the hangar, and Ramos pulled into the parking area. But instead of parking there, he pulled around to the back of the building and stopped.

Jumping out of the car, he grabbed his rifle, making sure he still had plenty of ammo. Sloan had left her rifle at the site, but she pulled out her handgun and nodded. They crept to the back of the hangar, then circled around the side facing away from the building where no one could see them.

An older Antonov cargo plane sat near the hangar and faced the runway. Carlos and his men were busy unloading the truck and carrying the crates to the plane. Ramos could see that the pilots were inside the cockpit. He might still have a chance to stop them once the weapons and his crate were all loaded, as long as he was close enough to be in range.

He ducked into the hangar, with Sloan following behind, and took refuge behind a parked car. Carlos supervised the men unloading the truck, gesturing at them to hurry. Ramos knew the only way to stop them was to disable the plane or get to the pilot. But, from here, it didn't look like that would be possible. There were too many of them, and he didn't like the odds. That meant he'd have to go with his backup plan.

"Come on," Sloan said, slipping out from behind the car, and running in a crouch toward the truck.

"Wait," Ramos said, swearing under his breath. Without a backward glance, she kept moving, and he knew if they were spotted, it was all over. Clenching his jaw, he followed closely behind, hoping he could stop her before she got them killed.

Sloan crouched down at the front end of the truck, and Ramos dropped down beside her. Before he could tell her to go back, one of Carlos's men came around to open the door. The man paused, then continued toward them.

Ramos jumped up, slamming the butt of his rifle into the man's gut, then across his jaw. As he went down, another man heard the commotion and came running.

"I'll get Carlos," Sloan said, and she took off around the other side of the truck.

Ramos shot the man coming toward him and rounded the end of the truck. Before he could get another shot off, a guard jumped from the truck bed in front of him, taking him by surprise. Ramos rushed into him, grabbing his wrist and twisting before he could shoot. The man yelled in pain, dropping his weapon. Ramos kept the momentum going and threw him to the ground.

Another man jumped from the back of the truck and swung his fist toward Ramos's face. Ramos ducked as several shots rang out. Then he side-stepped his attacker and landed a one-two punch to the man's head, dropping him to the ground.

Ramos couldn't see Carlos anywhere, but the shots came from the other side of the hangar where Sloan had run. Two men started shooting at him, and he ducked down beside the truck for cover. He rose to fire, but the men had moved out of sight.

He stood to follow, keeping low, and made it to the edge of the truck before he caught sight of Carlos. He held Sloan with an arm around her neck in a choke hold, and had a gun pointed to her head.

"Stop, or I kill her!"

Chapter 5

"Drop your gun or she dies!"

Ramos's mouth went dry. His chances of survival just went down the drain. If he gave up now, they were both dead, but what choice did he have?

"Do it now!" Carlos screamed.

Ramos caught Sloan's gaze. She pressed her lips together and shook her head, signaling him not to do it. He knew she could get out of Carlos's choke hold, but she needed a diversion so Carlos wouldn't pull the trigger.

Deciding his surrender might give her a chance, Ramos lifted both arms up, but held onto his gun, ready to take action.

A cold, hard, gun barrel pressed against the back of his head, and Ramos's breath caught.

"Should I kill him?"

"If anyone's going to kill him, it will be me!" Carlos breathed heavily and stared at Ramos. He shoved Sloan into another man's grasp and raised his gun to fire. He held it steady, but hesitated. Then he lowered it and narrowed his eyes. "But...I have a better idea. Tie them up. They're coming with us."

Carlos's men didn't waste any time. They relieved both Ramos and Sloan of all their weapons, making them remove their bullet-proof vests, which the gunmen happily took for themselves. Pulling Ramos's hands behind his back, they roughly tied him up and shoved him onto the ground next to Sloan.

They quickly finished loading the cargo onto the plane, killing any hope that Sloan's people would get there in time. Soon, Ramos and Sloan were pushed onto the floor of the plane beside the crates. As Ramos sat down, he gritted his teeth against the pain to his ribs. A few minutes later, the plane began to taxi down the runway.

"I'm sorry I got you into this," Sloan whispered. "I should've known he'd double-cross us."

"It was me he double-crossed. I guess my reputation wasn't enough to stop him. Any idea why he didn't kill us?"

Sloan didn't answer, and Ramos turned his head to catch her gaze. "You might as well tell me now. It can't get any worse."

She shook her head and let out a breath. "I'm so sorry. I should have told you."

Ramos sighed. That didn't sound good. He didn't prod, waiting patiently for Sloan to finally tell him what it was she'd been hiding all this time.

"There's a bounty on your head. I guess Carlos decided that he might as well collect it."

Ramos's eyes widened. "And you didn't think I needed to know this?"

"I didn't think...well, maybe I thought it would help him decide to make the deal with you. Not that I ever thought he'd be able to collect. I just thought that it might be an added incentive for him to make the deal. I thought I had it all covered. I thought I could protect you, and...I never thought it would turn out this way." She shook her head, and let out a moan of frustration. "This is all my fault."

Ramos's jaw clenched with anger. He should have known that he couldn't trust her. Now look at where they were. Of course, things might have turned out differently if he'd told her about his backup plan, so that was on him. If there was a bounty on his head...it meant that they literally planned to behead him. Carlos would probably ask to do it, and his stomach churned with sick dread.

The plane leveled out, and Carlos came back to gloat, sitting on a crate in front of them. "The mighty Ramos has fallen. And now I will finally have revenge for my brother's death. I wonder how much they'll give me for your head?"

If he was hoping to rattle Ramos, it didn't work, and Carlos's mouth turned into a grimace. "I didn't really need to keep you alive, but the money will be so much better if they can watch." He glanced at Sloan. "So can you. Or maybe they'll want you dead first? I don't know how much they'll give me for you, but when I tell them who you are, I think they will pay well."

Sloan's eyes widened, and Carlos smirked. "Yes...I know who you are. You even have a name...*Bella Rebelde*, beautiful rebel. Your head will look nice next to his, don't you think?"

He glanced at his men, then caught her gaze. "Haven't you been wondering where Antonio was?" At her raised brows, he smiled. "Oh...I see. You hadn't even noticed he was missing. Well, after your little rendezvous with him yesterday, I started to get suspicious. Then, when Ramos seemed to know who you were, I thought it was time I had a little chat with Antonio. He told me all about your plans to set me up...before he died."

With that, Carlos stood and smiled down at Sloan, enjoying the anger and pain that filled her eyes. Then he caught Ramos's hard gaze, and the smile left his face. "You will be dead soon enough."

Ramos didn't blink, holding Carlos's gaze with contempt. With a huff, Carlos shook his head and returned to the comfort of his seat.

Letting out a breath, Ramos glanced at Sloan. Her eyes had filled with tears. As they coursed down her cheeks, anger filled Ramos's heart. He knew nothing he could say would help Sloan feel better, so he scooted close to her until their shoulders touched. She sniffed, then blinked the tears from her eyes, and leaned her head against his shoulder.

Ramos wanted to tell her about his contingency plan, but he didn't want to get her hopes up in case he couldn't pull it off. Still, he vowed to do everything in his power to stop Carlos, even he had to die in the process.

"Sloan," Ramos said. "There's something I need you to do."

She sat up straight, and her brows drew together. "What?"

"I have a small blade in my boot, but I can't reach it. Do you think you can try?"

"Sure." She glanced into the plane at the men. "Let's scoot closer to that crate so they can't see us as well."

The cargo plane was noisy enough that they didn't have to worry about being quiet. Soon, Ramos had scrunched against the crate with his knees bent, and Sloan had turned, so her hands could reach his boots.

"There's a thin blade inside the boot by my ankle. It's right behind my anklebone."

"Okay. I've got to get a little closer."

With her hands tied behind her back, she couldn't see what she was doing, so it took a while to find the right spot.

Ramos guided her, while keeping a watch on Carlos and his men.

"Is that it?" she asked.

"Yes. It has a ridge on the end. Make sure you hold onto it tight while you pull it out." As she leaned forward, he held his breath, hoping she wouldn't drop it. "You've got about three more inches on the shaft before you reach the blade, so don't worry about cutting yourself."

"Good to know."

The blade finally cleared his boot, and he sighed with relief. "It's sharp, so turn it carefully so you don't get cut. I'll tell you when it's safe to start sawing through the rope." She turned the blade in her nimble fingers, until it was pointed in the right direction. "Good. Now you can start cutting."

The sharp blade cut through the rope quickly, and soon she was free. As she pulled the rope from her hands, he glanced at Carlos's men, relieved that none of them had looked their way.

He twisted to give Sloan a better angle, and pain from his ribs shot into his side like a hot iron. He managed to hold back a groan, but it was close. She quickly cut through his bonds, and he straightened, letting out a relieved breath.

"What now?" she asked.

He took the blade and put it back in his boot. "We can't let them know we're free until after we land, so we need to pretend we're still tied up." He wrapped the rope around one of his wrists and hoped it was enough to fool them. "After we land, and they're busy unloading, we'll make our move."

"Okay."

"Wait for my signal this time."

Sloan pursed her lips, but nodded, leaving Ramos grateful that she hadn't argued. She scooted back to her place beside him, moving her hands behind her back, and Ramos did the same.

Just then, one of Carlos's men stood and glanced in their direction. Ramos stared back at him, his lips in a grim line and his gaze narrowed, almost daring him to come closer. The man stiffened and looked away, then sat back down, and didn't glance toward Ramos again.

It took close to three hours before the plane began its descent, plenty of time to make it to Mexico. Ramos sat up straight and nudged Sloan, who had been resting her head on his shoulder.

"We're landing."

She straightened, then made sure her hands looked like they were still tied behind her back. Soon, the plane touched ground, and they taxied to a stop. Ramos wasn't sure how many men would be waiting for Carlos, and his lips set in grim determination for what would happen next.

Even with their hands loose, they were outnumbered, and it would take a small miracle to survive. At least he'd go down fighting, much better than what Carlos had planned.

The cargo door opened, and Carlos and his men hurried toward the opening. It was full dark outside, but overhead lights from the hangar showed a truck and two cars, along with five men. At least, in the dark, he hoped no one would see that his hands weren't bound.

Carlos glanced at Ramos and Sloan with a satisfied sneer on his face. "Get them up," he commanded one of his men.

As the guard pulled Ramos to his feet, Ramos kept a tight hold on the rope to keep his hands together. He staggered a bit after sitting for so long, and pain raced through his side, but he held back a groan. After the guard got Sloan to her feet, he took hold of their upper arms and led them out of the plane.

"Take them into the hangar while we unload," Carlos said. "And don't let them out of your sight."

Inside the hangar, the guard motioned for them to sit on the ground in full view of the unloading process. He then stood beside them, watching the men unload the crates. Ramos kept a furtive eye on the guard, relieved to find that his attention rested on the crates, and he hardly spared them a second glance.

Ramos hoped he stayed distracted long enough to make his move, but he had to wait for the right moment. It took close to twenty minutes for the men to load up the truck. Once it was full, the men secured the door and climbed inside the cab. Several men got in one car, leaving the other one for Carlos and the man standing guard.

As the driver started the truck, Carlos glanced in their direction. The man guarding them walked the distance to Carlos's side, and Ramos knew this was his only chance to put his plan into action. Moving fast, he reached to his foot and twisted off the heel of his boot. A small remote fell into his hand.

He replaced the heel and glanced at Sloan, then tapped in the sequence of numbers and pushed the button, hoping that it worked how his friend had promised.

All at once, a huge explosion rocked the ground. The truck rose in the air and blew apart, setting off a chain reaction of fire that exploded the weapons, sending up a massive fireball into the black sky.

Bits and pieces of debris showered down on them and the surrounding area. Both cars blew up, and Ramos grabbed Sloan to pull her deeper into the hangar, hoping it would protect them.

More explosions rocked the ground while Ramos and Sloan held their arms over their heads. Ramos glanced toward the devastation and caught sight of Carlos staggering to his feet. One of his arms dangled loosely at his side, and blood covered the side of his face.

As he stepped toward the relative safety of the hangar, the plane burst into flames, shooting fire, debris, and billowing smoke into the air. The blast with its shredding fragments knocked Carlos to the ground, and he didn't move again.

A part of the truck came to rest beside the hangar and burned with fierce heat. Soon, fire raced up the side of the building. As smoke poured into the hangar, Sloan gasped at the destruction. "We have to get out of here!"

Ramos nodded and took Sloan's arm. In a crouching run, they rushed out of the building, passing Carlos on their way. Ramos paused to glance at the blackened and disfigured man. Carlos opened his mouth to say something, but no sound came out. Then Sloan tugged at Ramos's arm, and he turned away, eager to leave this place behind.

They ran into the darkness, following a dirt road until they were out of breath and panting. In the distance, the fire burned bright, sending a bright orange glow into the darkness. Stopping to rest, Sloan turned to him. "How did you do that?"

Ramos held his side, panting heavily. "I added a crate of C4 to the mix. It was my contingency plan in case something went wrong."

Sloan exhaled. "My boss is going to kill me."

Ramos nodded his agreement. "But at least you're still alive."

"That all depends," she responded. "It looks to me like we're out in the middle of nowhere."

"Yes," Ramos agreed. "But we have a road to follow that should lead us somewhere." They began walking, but more slowly this time, giving Ramos a chance to catch his breath. Soon the pain in his ribs subsided, and he breathed easier.

"It doesn't look like anyone's coming," Sloan said. "That surprises me after such a huge explosion."

"I know," Ramos said. "But I imagine the cartels down here have all kinds of secret places for their airstrips, and the further from civilization, the better."

"True, but I'd sure like to know where we are." Sloan rubbed her arms against the chill. "At least it's not as cold here as it would be at home."

As they rounded a bend, a glimmer of lights shone in the distance, and Sloan clapped. "Look." In her excitement, she clasped Ramos around the waist and held him tight. He would have enjoyed the contact more if it didn't hurt his cracked ribs. But he wasn't about to tell Sloan that.

"We're not out of the woods yet. Any idea how we're going to get back home?" he asked.

Sloan pulled away. "I have several contacts in Mexico. If I can use a phone, or if we can make it to the embassy in Mexico City, I'm sure I can get us home."

"Even a hit-man like me?"

"Yes...of course."

They walked in silence for several minutes before Sloan spoke again. "Thanks, Ramos. Even though I'll probably get re-assigned, or worse, fired, I'm glad you blew up the truck and all the weapons...along with Carlos and his men."

Ramos mumbled an agreement, happy to let her do all the talking, since he was still smarting that she hadn't been truthful with him.

"What surprised me the most was the helicopter," she continued. "Who would have thought he'd ever pull something like that?"

"Carlos was more cunning than either of us gave him credit for."

"Maybe," she said, stopping to face him. "But you outsmarted him...and me. You saved us both, so I guess I owe you one."

Ramos nodded. "Yes. I think you do."

She had the grace to duck her head. "I'm sorry I didn't tell you everything. It was a mistake, and it won't happen again."

He was sure of that, since he didn't plan on ever helping her again, no matter how nicely she asked.

"Ramos, really...I'm sorry." Her gaze caught his. In the starlight, her eyes glistened. "You have every right to hate me, but please believe that I'd never do anything to hurt you. I admit that it was probably a mistake to involve you in this, but...I wanted to see you again, and this seemed like a perfect excuse. You don't know how many times I've thought of you these last few months. We shared something special, and I wanted to see if it was still there."

He huffed out a breath, then gave in and wrapped his arms around her. As she clung to him, he closed his eyes, savoring the feel of her body next to his. "We did have something special, but I'm not sure it could ever go anywhere. We're both in the wrong line of work, don't you think?"

"You could stop working for Manetto."

His breath caught, and he stepped out of her grasp. "Babe. That's not going to happen." He held her gaze, willing her to understand that he meant every word. Finally, she dropped her head and nodded.

They continued down the road, each lost in their own thoughts. A moment later, the rumble of a vehicle coming toward them broke the silence. "We'd better get off the road," Ramos said.

They hurried into the scraggly bushes beside the road and got down on their stomachs. Soon, a couple of trucks passed them. Ramos counted at least five occupants sitting in the back of each truck, most holding rifles. He was grateful it was still dark, but he knew they needed to get to safety before the sun came up.

"What do you think?" he asked Sloan. "More soldiers, or the police?"

"I don't know. But I think they're probably looking for Carlos and his shipment. So we need to be careful."

They got back on the road and kept walking. An hour passed, and the sky lightened. As the sun began to rise in the East, Ramos and Sloan stepped into the little town. At an open gas station, they stopped to find out where they were. Sloan spoke to the owner in perfect Spanish, and Ramos let her do all the talking.

After a few minutes, she turned to him. "We're about fifty miles out of Mexico City. You don't happen to have any money in those boots of yours, do you?"

He smiled. "I always have money on me."

Her eyes lit up. "Great, because he says he has an old motorcycle he'll sell us. How much have you got?"

"I need to see the motorcycle first," Ramos said. "Then we can make a deal."

Sloan shrugged, and the man led them around to the back. Ramos scanned the area closely, his instincts on high alert for an attack. Satisfied that they were safe, he glanced at the pile of junk the man had taken them to see.

The man pulled an old blanket from the bike, sending a cloud of dust into the air. Ramos frowned. Was this guy trying to take advantage of them? The man wrestled the bike out of the pile and dusted it off with a rag he pulled from his back pocket. Grime covered the body and black leather seat, which only looked slightly better once he got done.

Sloan spoke to the man, questioning him about whether or not it even worked. She also pointed out that the back tire was flat, but he told her he could pump it up.

The name on the gas tank caught Ramos's attention, and everything else faded into the background. It was a Triumph, and not just any Triumph, but a Bonneville Triumph. It even looked like one of the first ever made, which would put it around 1959. A vintage classic.

Of course, that didn't mean it would run, but a sense of excitement washed over him just the same. The man pushed it around to an air compressor and filled up the tire, then added gas to the tank before heading inside to get the key.

Ramos examined the engine, frame, front and rear suspension, along with the chain, muffler, and brake levers. It had twin pipes and twin carburetors and, if everything worked, it was powerful enough to get them where they needed to go. But he wouldn't know if it worked until he started it up.

Returning with the key, the man handed it over. Ramos inserted it, then pulled in the clutch and put the bike in neutral. Next, he turned on the choke and pulled out the kick starter. He quickly pushed down on the starter while giving it a little gas.

It didn't work the first time, so he tried it again. By the third time, the engine caught, and he revved it a few times before it settled into the kind of purr that he liked to hear. "I'm taking it for a spin."

Before Sloan could say a word, he put it in first and hit the road. He shifted through each gear before making a U-turn and heading back. It wasn't as smooth as it could be, but it ran pretty well for sitting in a pile of junk.

He came to a stop in front of Sloan and turned it off, then checked the oil. Finally satisfied, he nodded. Deciding to let the man think he couldn't speak Spanish, he glanced at Sloan. "Tell him it needs some oil. If he can add that, I'll take it."

After Sloan spoke to the man, he took Ramos's measure before coming up with a price. The man asked for eight-hundred dollars, and Ramos let Sloan translate to give him more time to decide what to do. Eight-hundred was a steal, but he had to negotiate on the price so the guy wouldn't feel like he'd been cheated.

"Offer him six-hundred."

Sloan did, and the man shook his head, repeating eight-hundred or no deal. Ramos had to give the guy credit for sticking to his price. He might have haggled a little more, but they were running out of time. "Tell him I'll take it."

At the man's happy smile, Ramos kept up the disgruntled act, and opened one of his pockets. He slipped his hand inside the lining and pulled out a flat bill wallet of one-hundred dollar bills. He counted out eight of them and slid the rest back in his pocket before handing the money over.

After the man added some oil, and topped off the tank with gas, Ramos started her up. With Sloan's arms wrapped around his waist, he took off down the road. He enjoyed the feel of the breeze through his hair, and hope surged in his heart that they just might make it out of there alive.

They reached Mexico City by mid-morning. Sloan directed him to the embassy, and he pulled to a stop.

"So what happens now?" Ramos asked.

"I need to report in and let my director know what happened. I'm sure once everything is straightened out I can get us home, but it will probably take some time, maybe even a day or two."

Ramos raised his brows. This wasn't a scenario he liked. If he had a passport, he'd leave her there and get a flight home on his own.

She noticed his hesitation and drew a quick breath to explain. "I know you don't want to wait, but I'm sure you'll be fine. Besides, you'll need a passport to get back to the states. I can arrange it all and get us on the next flight home."

"Sure," Ramos said. "But if it's all the same to you, I'll wait out here." He glanced down the street to the nearest open food court. "I'll be over there. When you're done, just come and find me."

Sloan's eyes widened. "Uh...can't you just come with me? You can corroborate my story. It's standard procedure, and I promise nothing's going to happen to you. I really need you to come."

He sent her a smile and shook his head. "Sorry Sloan, but I'd rather not. Don't worry, I'm not going anywhere. If you need me, just come find me."

Her shoulders sagged with disappointment. "Are you sure?" He nodded, and she let out a frustrated breath. "Fine. Just promise me you'll be there when I'm done."

He shrugged. "Where am I going to go? I need that passport, and I'll come in if you really need me to."

She nodded, but her brows drew together with uncertainty. She sent him one more pleading glance that did nothing to change his mind. Defeated, she sighed and started toward the building. Just before entering, she turned. Ramos gave her a nod, then pulled the bike away from the curb and headed toward the vendors.

That was close. He hated lying to her, but there was no way he was going inside that building. Who knew what they would do to him? It would be easy to put him in a holding cell and ask questions later, and he wasn't about to risk his freedom for anything.

He followed the slow-moving traffic and kept watch for someplace to buy a phone. A few minutes later, he parked the bike on the street and hurried inside a store. He bought a pre-paid phone, along with some sunglasses, and stuck it in his pocket.

Then he finally gave into his growling stomach, unable to resist the delicious smells. Finding a street vendor in the Distrito Federal section of the city, he bought a couple of tacos sudados and delicious frutas en tacha.

After wolfing them down, he found a semi-private spot and put the call through to Manetto.

"Where the hell are you?" Manetto asked.

"Mexico City," Ramos answered. "I ran into a few snags, and I'm afraid I didn't get the money, but Carlos is dead, along with most of his men. Only problem was, I had to blow up all the weapons."

"Hmm...I doubt that went over well with Sloan."

"Exactly. That's why I dropped her off at the embassy. She's there now and claims she can get me a passport and a ride out of here. But I'm not so sure I want her help, especially with all the strings that come with it."

"I'll send my jet. Can you get to the airstrip we used before?"

Ramos let out a relieved breath. "Yes. I've got transportation, so that's not a problem."

"Good. I'll call you at this number once the plane is in the air."

Chapter 6

Ramos knew it would take him a couple of hours to get to the airstrip. Then he'd probably have to wait another two hours before the plane landed. That gave him some time before he had to leave the city. If he could talk to an old friend who lived here, there might be a chance he could find out who was responsible for the bounty on his head.

Since Manuel was most likely at his car dealership at this time of day, he headed to the lower city district to find him. Once he reached the car lot, he parked across the street to observe. Manuel came out to talk to some people, then went back inside, and Ramos made his move.

He rode the bike to the back of the lot and parked behind the building, then strode inside, going straight to Manuel's office which overlooked the car lot. Manuel sat at his desk, writing on some paperwork, so Ramos paused inside the doorway and folded his arms.

Manuel glanced up, and then jerked with surprise. "Ramos. What the hell! You about gave me a heart attack."

Ramos smiled, glad he'd had that effect. "I was in the neighborhood and thought I'd stop by. It's been a while since I was here."

"Sí, mi amigo. It has." Manuel's brows drew together, and he glanced out the window toward the lot. "But you should probably leave town. It's not safe for you here."

"I got that already." Ramos nodded. "That's why I'm here. You wouldn't happen to know who put the bounty on my head, would you?"

Manuel shrugged. "It's not exactly a secret, so I don't suppose it will do me any harm to tell you. As long as you don't pass it along that I did."

Ramos spread his hands. "Manuel. We're friends. You know that."

"Sí, I am hoping so."

"Both Manetto and I will owe you a favor, and you know we take care of our own."

Manuel nodded, then stood and motioned for Ramos to come in and sit down, making sure the door was closed for privacy. "Very well," he began. "You must know that the demise of Gonzales was a particular loss for the chief of police, who received many favors from the Gonzales Cartel. So, a few months ago, and with the promptings of a few highly placed officials, he spread the word of a bounty on your head."

"What's his name?"

"Inspector Salazar. He has been known to take bribes and share the spoils from the ransoms of hostages."

"Do you have a phone number for him?"

"Of course. You can call the police station and ask for him." Manuel shuffled through his desk to find a phone book. "It is here. I will write it down for you."

"Thank you Manuel. You've been extremely helpful. I'll make sure you're compensated."

Manuel handed the note with the number on it to Ramos and shrugged. "It is nothing, but of course I appreciate doing business with you. I hope you do not confront him alone. He has many friends."

Ramos stuffed the paper into his pocket and stood. "Don't worry. I hope you hear that the bounty no longer exists by this time tomorrow. If you don't, please let me know."

"I will let you know, either way."

They said their goodbyes, and Ramos left Manuel's office, heading out the back to his motorcycle. The police station wasn't far, but he didn't need to talk to Salazar face-to-face for what he had in mind.

He knew Salazar. In fact, he'd spoken with him the last time he'd been in Mexico. He also knew that Salazar was the same man who had tried to get Shelby to pay a ransom for Manetto. It would be nice to take him out but, for now, he hoped a threat would do.

He rode past the station, then turned down an alley on the other side of the street and parked. He climbed up the fire-escape on the side of the building and pulled himself to the roof. If he remembered correctly, Salazar's office was on the third floor, with big windows overlooking the street.

From his perch, he had a good view of the office, but it was empty. He watched, waiting for his chance, and was rewarded a short time later when Salazar entered and sat at the desk.

Ramos pulled out his phone and called the station. Speaking in perfect Spanish, he asked for his good friend, Chief Inspector Salazar. He watched Salazar pick up the phone and heard him say his name.

"Salazar," Ramos began. "I see you are wearing your red tie today. If you don't want it to get ruined, I suggest you keep still."

"Who is this?"

"Have you heard what happened to Carlos early this morning? He brought me here to collect on a bounty that you put out on me. Now, I've got you in my sights, and I'm ready to pull the trigger, but I might be persuaded to let you live...if you take the bounty off my head."

Salazar inhaled sharply. "Ramos?" He pulled a drawer open.

"Keep your hands on your desk. Now. You know what? I'm running out of time. Maybe I'll just take the shot and be done with..."

"No! I will rescind the bounty. You have my word."

"Good," Ramos said. "And believe me, if I hear it hasn't been rescinded, or another bounty is ever taken out on me again, you will be the first to die." He quickly disconnected and hurried off the roof. As he dropped to the ground, he noticed a policeman rushing out of the building and glancing up at the rooftop.

Not wasting time, Ramos hopped on the bike, started her up, and continued through the alley to the other side of the street. He heard yelling from somewhere behind him and only slowed a little to make the turn. Coming out on the street in a rush, he masterfully avoided hitting several cars.

He sped up between lights, then slowed and turned down another road, finally circling out to the main highway and taking the fifty-seven toward San Miguel. Safely on the freeway without a tail, he breathed easier and hoped his bluff had worked on Salazar. If not, he knew he'd be back.

It took him an hour and a half to get to the small airfield. Manetto had contacted the lone operator of the airstrip, so he was expecting Ramos. The man offered him water and food, along with a place on the couch to close his eyes.

Ramos gratefully accepted. He reclined on the sofa, and pulled up his shirt to take a look at his ribs. The right side of his chest where Carlos's shot had hit his vest was black and blue. From the pain, he knew his ribs were probably cracked.

There wasn't much he could do about his cracked ribs except take something for the pain. But, since he didn't know the airstrip operator, he decided to wait until he got on the plane to find some aspirin. He pulled his shirt back down, and took the bottle of water the operator handed him.

They spoke for a few minutes, then the operator left him to rest. After a night without sleep, it was tempting to close his eyes, but Ramos wasn't about to leave his life in the hands of a stranger, no matter how well Manetto was paying him.

Fighting exhaustion, Ramos managed to stay awake, even offering to play chess with the operator, who was more than happy to oblige, especially since Ramos lost every game. The sky began to darken. Just as he thought he couldn't keep his eyes open a moment longer, he caught sight of the plane coming in for a landing.

Relief coursed through him. He'd made it. As the plane taxied up to the small building, Ramos stood, swaying a little from exhaustion.

The door opened, and Ricky rushed out, a big smile on his face. "Hey man. Good to see you. Manetto sent me along in case you needed me."

"Thanks for coming."

"No problem."

Ramos hated leaving the motorcycle behind. Then he had an idea. "Do you think we can get the bike on the plane?"

"Hell, yeah."

In the end, they needed both the pilot and the operator's help, but they still managed to get the bike onboard.

Unfortunately, it didn't help Ramos's ribs any. He practically fell onto the leather seat. After pushing the button so that it shifted into a reclining position, he promptly fell asleep.

Three days later, Ramos sat in the conference room at Thrasher Development. He was the only one there since it was Christmas Eve, and he had to get the bonuses ready. Tonight, Manetto had a nice dinner planned at his club for his most trusted associates.

As he placed one of the checks in an envelope, he glanced up to find Shelby standing in the doorway. "Hi," she said, her voice sounding breathless. "How are you?"

It always cheered him up to find Shelby a little speechless around him. "I'm good."

"Jackie told me you ran into some problems with Carlos."

"Yes. It was a fiasco, but I made it back in one piece."

"What happened?" His mind immediately centered on the explosion, and Shelby gasped. "Holy hell!"

He chuckled, then sent her a smile. "I don't think I'll be going back to Mexico anytime soon."

"So did Sloan make it out too?"

"Yeah." He shrugged. "I mean, I don't know for sure, since I left her at the embassy." He told Shelby the abbreviated version of what happened, but it was easy to see that she picked up the rest from his mind, because her face paled when he mentioned the bounty on his head.

Shelby's breath caught. "They were going to behead you? Oh my gosh! Don't you ever help her again."

He smiled, pleased that she was so outraged on his behalf. He also managed to keep the news that the bounty had been rescinded from his mind. He knew it was a devious thing to do, but he liked how concerned she was about him, and he didn't want her to stop. "I'm not planning on it."

"Good." She took a breath and let it out. "Uh...I came for my bonus check. Uncle Joey asked me to stop by since I'm not going to his big dinner tonight."

"Sure. It's right here." He picked it up and stepped around the table to hand it to her. Someone had put a sprig of mistletoe above the door, and he hoped that if he got her to take a few steps back...

Shelby caught her breath, then desire darkened her eyes, and his heart picked up speed. Was she really going to let him kiss her?

A laugh escaped her lips, and she stepped out of his reach. "No. I'm not. But I did bring you a Christmas present." She pulled a small box from her purse and held it out to him.

"Thanks." The last gift she'd given him was a handmade watch, and he loved it, especially the engraving on the back where she'd called him her "hero." He liked being her hero...and that she admired him so much.

"Just open it up and quit teasing me."

With a grin, he pulled the ribbon off the box and took off the lid. Inside, he found a circular, black leather key fob with a silver skull inside, and the words, "Harley-Davidson Motorcycles" stamped around the skull. "Babe...this is great. I like the skull."

Shelby smiled. "It reminded me of you. The skull, I mean. Because it's...you know...uh cool...like that guy in the comics."

He chuckled. "You mean the one that looks like a devil with his skull-head all in flames?" He laughed some more, thinking that he liked it, and wondered if Shelby realized that it fit with her hero image of him, just like the watch.

"Hmmm...I guess you have a point, although you have to admit it goes with the Harley, right?" She caught his gaze, and her eyes widened. "Your motorcycle is a Harley, isn't it?"

"Yeah, babe. You got it right."

"Phew. Good. Well...I'd better go. I'm really glad you made it back in one piece."

"Me too." He could tell she was real tempted to give him a hug, so he pulled her into his arms before she could protest. "Thanks, Shelby. Have a Merry Christmas." He held her close, enjoying this small moment of intimacy.

After taking a deep breath, she pulled away and backed out of the door. "Uh...bye."

He smiled, noting the pink flush on her face. She hurried toward the doors like she was trying to escape a hot blaze that was about to burn her up. At the last minute, he called to her. "Shelby."

"Huh?"

"You forgot something." He held up the envelope with her Christmas bonus.

"Oh! Right." Her eyes widened, and she hurried back to get it.

Ramos moved forward but stopped right under the mistletoe and worked hard to make sure his thoughts were blocked from her mind. He held the envelope out and waited.

Just before reaching him, Shelby jerked to a stop and her gaze narrowed, then she shook her head and looked him over from top to bottom. "You really are a devil in a black suit. Hey...isn't that a real song? If I didn't know better, I'd think it was written about you."

He laughed, then shrugged and handed her the envelope, knowing that every time he looked at his new key fob, he'd think of her. "Bye Shelby."

This time she made it all the way out the door, leaving him with a big grin on his face.

He finished up his task, then gathered up the envelopes and slipped on his coat to head to the club. They always closed the club on Christmas Eve for their special gathering, and Ramos looked forward to the nice spread Manetto provided.

He also looked forward to spending Christmas day with his neighbor and his family. They always had excellent food, and their kids adored him. He realized just how much he needed a break from his job, along with some time to unwind and be a normal person.

At the club, he unlocked the door in the back and walked down the short hall before entering the main room. Inside, he flipped on the lights and smiled to find the room completely different. Jackie always hired caterers for the food, but she had several of the round tables nicely decorated with tablecloths and candles.

He shrugged out of his coat, hanging it on a rack, and walked around the room to set the envelopes with the bonuses at the head of the table where Manetto would be sitting.

A sharp knock sounded at the main door, and he frowned. He knew the closed sign was posted, so who could it be? It came again, so he hurried to the door and pushed the curtain aside to see who it was.

Sloan stood on the other side. "Let me in," she said.

Surprised, he unlocked the door and pulled it open. As she came in, he glanced at the car parked at the curb and noticed that someone sat inside. "Who's in the car?" he asked, closing the door.

"My partner." Sloan rubbed her hands together and smiled up at him. "I can only stay for a minute, but I had to come back to clean out the apartment, and I saw the lights come on, so I took a chance that you'd be here."

"You have a partner now?"

Sloan blew out a breath. "Yeah. My director wasn't too happy about the way everything went down in Mexico, so I'm not on my own anymore." He nodded and she continued. "I felt bad that I didn't get to say goodbye. But I don't blame you for leaving. It was probably a good thing. I mean...even though we did lose the weapons, and a couple of our guys got shot, I think the message got through."

Ramos smiled and nodded. "Yes, I think leaving a crater in the ground would have that effect."

"Yeah, so it wasn't a total failure. And Carlos isn't a problem anymore. So we did well." She pulled a card from her jacket and handed it over.

"What's this?"

"It's my card with my number. I told you I'd owe you a favor, so here's my card in case you need me."

"Right." Ramos put the card in his pocket and held her gaze. "Is that it?"

"No," she stammered. "Remember that I told you I had a Christmas present for you?"

"I remember we made a deal."

She nodded. "Yeah, and since it was a success, I'm here to give you your present."

He glanced at her expectantly, but she just stood there without a package in sight. "Okay."

"It's not exactly something I can wrap up, but I think it's something that you'll be happy to get."

He caught a hint of unease from her. "Then why are you so nervous to tell me? Are you sure I'll like it?"

She hesitated, but nodded and then shrugged. "Well, yeah. I would want to know."

"Know what?" His stomach tightened. What had she done?

"Remember those papers you found in the apartment? The ones with your name on them?"

He took a breath, unsure where she was going with this. "Yes."

"As you know, I did some digging into your background, and I found out something about your father."

His brows rose in surprise. "My father?"

"Yes. I remember you telling me that he disappeared when you were a kid; right after you came to the U.S. from Cuba. So I did some research. Ramos...I found out that he was taken back to Cuba against his will. He might still be alive."

Shock ran over him. All these years, he'd thought his father was dead. Could it be true? "Are you sure you got the name right?"

"It's Rafael Ramirez, isn't it?"

Ramos nodded, barely hearing her give him his father's date of birth, and the date they'd entered the U.S. "Yes. That's right. At least the day we came to the states is right. I barely remember his birth date, but it was in the fall, so that sounds right, too. But why would someone force him back to Cuba?"

She let out a breath. "You don't know much about your father, do you?" He raised his brows, and she continued. "He worked for the government, possibly in the military. I don't know a lot, but I think he was pretty high up in the regime's ruling members. Maybe there was a falling out and he fled. Or, it could be another reason entirely, but I do know that he was taken back against his will."

It took a minute for Ramos to take in what she'd said. His father had worked for the Cuban government? How could that be true? His mother had never mentioned anything like that. If his father had worked for them and left, and they'd taken him back for some political reason, it couldn't have ended well.

"Then it would be a miracle if he had survived. Do you have any evidence that he's still alive?" Ramos knew in his heart that his father would have done everything in his power to come back to his family. That meant something bad had happened to him.

"Not right now. If they put him in prison, it would be highly unlikely after all these years, but you never know." She shrugged. "Anyway, I thought it would be nice that you knew he didn't leave you or your family willingly."

He glanced at her and nodded, but he'd always known that his father would never have left them willingly, and knowing he was taken hadn't changed a thing. "So you did all of this searching just for me?"

She bit her lip. "Yes. I thought it might be nice for you to have some closure...and I have contacts because of my job."

Was that the truth? Or was there something else there as well? "So there's no way to find out what happened to him?"

"Maybe...I'm not supposed to talk about this, but there's a slight chance they might send me to Cuba in the near future. If that ever happens, I promise to look into it for you."

Ramos nodded. Even though it was a long shot, he couldn't help the feeling of hope that rose in his chest. On impulse, he asked, "Could you take me with you?" At her raised brows, he continued. "It would help make up for not getting a dime from Carlos."

She laughed. "Yeah, right. You're lucky I told Wells that blowing everything up was my contingency plan and not yours. Otherwise, he might have thrown you in the clinker."

Ramos's lips turned down. "Is that so?"

"No...I'm just kidding, but it's probably a good idea if I don't mention you for a while. Anyway...just let me do my thing, and I'll keep in touch. And you can always call me about that favor."

"Okay, sure. Thanks Sloan."

She huffed out a breath and glanced at him with a frown. "Do you even know my first name?"

"You mean we're on a first name basis?" She rolled her eyes, so he continued. "Yes, your first name is Mia. I like it, but I like Sloan, too." She didn't respond, and he blew out a breath. "Don't tell me you want to start calling me Alejandro."

"I wouldn't dream of it," she said.

"Good." He let out an exaggerated breath, then inspiration struck. "I have a Christmas present for you, too."

"You do?"

He nodded. "Merry Christmas, Sloan." Ramos deliberately used her last name. Then he gathered her in his arms and kissed her soundly. It took her by surprise, but she soon kissed him back with more passion than he expected. It fanned the flames buried deep inside him, and got his blood boiling, letting him know that the old spark hadn't gone anywhere.

The honking of a horn brought him back to his senses and he pulled his lips from hers. Desire turned her eyes into dark fathomless pools, and she had trouble catching her breath. He released his hold on her, and she swayed before catching her balance, and stepping back.

"Till next time," he said, his gaze full of promise and his lips turned up in a teasing grin.

Her breath hitched with annoyance. Then she shook her head to clear it, and gave him a scorching look of her own before she turned and rushed out the door.

Part 2

Chapter 7

Ramos polished off the last of his eggs and hurried into the bathroom to finish getting ready for work. He was running a little late, but since he'd been staying at the apartment at Thrasher Development on the twenty-sixth floor, he was already there, minus the few steps through the door and down the hall.

In the last couple of months since Christmas, and his visit to Mexico with Sloan, not much had happened. He was grateful for the reprieve, since it had taken time for his cracked ribs, along with a few other injuries to heal. This morning, he'd made it through a killer workout, which meant he was ready for action.

Ramos wore his dark jeans with a slate blue shirt, his gun resting in the holster at his side. He shrugged on a navy blazer to complete the look and opened the door to the office. Heading down the hall, he passed the surveillance room and ducked inside.

As he scanned the monitors, a smile broke over his face to see Shelby in the elevator, looking at her reflection in the shiny metal doors. She put on her lipstick, and checked to see if any had gotten on her teeth. Then she smoothed down her hair and waited until the doors opened. She was wearing the black leather jacket he'd given her, along with black pants and boots.

He smiled. Just a few months ago, she'd complained about wearing black all the time. Now it seemed like it was second nature for her. It meant she was getting more comfortable working for Manetto, and Ramos wasn't going to grumble about that. Life before Shelby wasn't half as interesting as life after. She could get into trouble without even trying. It kept him on his toes, and he wouldn't want it any other way.

He left the room and came down the hall just as Shelby entered Thrasher Development. She glanced up at him, and he caught her gaze wandering appreciatively over his manly form. He sent a mental message of *I must look pretty good today*, and watched her face turn a sweet shade of pink.

"Um...uh..." She stammered. "Well, yeah..."

Ramos chuckled. "Thanks Shelby. You look pretty good, too." Then he thought, *and not one bit of lipstick on your teeth, either.*

Her brows drew together. "How did...you saw that?"

He shrugged and cleared his mind since he didn't want her to know he'd been spying on her in the elevator. "Just a lucky guess. I must have gotten it right, though."

"Yes...you did."

He smiled, and they started down the hallway to Manetto's office. "Are you ready for today?" Shelby nodded, but from her hesitation he could tell she wasn't too happy to be there. "Hey, this meeting should be easy. You probably won't even have to say anything."

"Oh. That's good to know. So how are things with you? Are the ribs all healed up?"

"Yes. I'm back to one hundred percent."

"Good to hear." Her forehead wrinkled with concern, and her lips quirked into a frown, but she didn't say anything.

"What?" he asked.

"Oh...I'm just...you know...concerned."

"About what?"

"Um...well...you haven't heard from Sloan lately, have you? Not that I'm prying or anything, but you know she hasn't got your best interests at heart, so I hope if you do hear from her, you'll tell her to get lost."

Ramos hid a smile. "No, I haven't heard from her." Then he thought *it's nice to know you care.*

She got a little flustered, but shrugged it off and smiled. "You know it."

They reached Manetto's door and strode inside, finding Manetto on the phone. He hung up and smiled at them. "Thanks for coming Shelby. Colin King will be here in a few minutes." He rubbed his hands together, and Ramos knew from experience that it meant he was looking forward to the meeting, especially with Shelby on his side.

"Let me tell you what this is all about," he began. "I'm thinking of selling a piece of property that I've been sitting on for a long time. I got an offer a few days ago from King's company to buy it. The location isn't the best for development, so I thought I might as well cash it in. But I want to know if he has any ulterior motives, and if it's a good idea."

"Okay," Shelby said. "Makes sense to me."

"Good. Let's sit down at the table."

While they got settled, Ramos stood at the door, watching for King. Manetto had told Ramos to stick around, just to make King sweat a little, and Ramos never objected to playing his part. Manetto had never met King, but his reputation as a slick operator had preceded him, and Manetto wanted to make sure King knew who was boss.

A moment later, King entered the office, wearing a business suit and sporting a short beard, heavily doused with gray. He carried a leather briefcase and walked in like he owned the place. Ramos could see that he was definitely someone who knew how to sweet talk his way around the business elite.

Ramos took an instant dislike to King's cocky attitude, but knowing Shelby would make mincemeat out of him lightened his animosity. Even so, Ramos wasn't about to be nice, and he sent King a hard stare before ushering him into the room.

Keeping up appearances, he stepped inside as well and shut the door behind them. Then he stood against the door with his feet braced in a watchful stance to set the tone. King sent him a wary glance before greeting Manetto.

"Thanks for coming," Manetto began, standing and offering his hand to shake. "This is one of my financial planners, Shelby Nichols."

By her widened eyes, Ramos knew that the introduction as a financial planner had taken Shelby by surprise. Which, considering her mind-reading abilities, was a hard thing to accomplish. Still, her lips turned up into a quick smile, and she graciously shook the hand he offered.

"Nice to meet you, Shelby," King said. "Who do you work for?"

Shelby's brows drew together in confusion. "Uh...him," she said, pointing to Manetto.

"Oh, of course," King said. "I just thought you might work for one of the investment firms as well, like Life Funding, or AmeriPrize?"

Shelby shook her head. "Nope. Just him."

"Let's take a look at your proposal," Manetto said, taking charge of the conversation. Ramos tried not to smile, but Shelby must have picked up his amusement because she sent him a frown. He winked at her, but otherwise kept a straight face. She glanced up at the ceiling, but kept from rolling her eyes, impressing him with her restraint.

King didn't waste any time. He pulled out a large file and proceeded to go over each page. Ramos could tell that King had done his research, and he brought some compelling facts in favor of the sale. Still, Ramos hoped Shelby picked up what was really going on, because this guy had to be hiding something.

After showing them the worth of comparable lots, and offering Manetto a sum of one-point-five million for his property, Shelby spoke up. "Why do you want this property so much?"

"I'm looking for investors to develop the area," King answered. "It's not much now, but I'm hoping in about one to two years I'll have a plan in place to attract a big company who's looking to expand. But before I can pitch it to anyone, I have to acquire the property. As I'm sure you're aware, this also means I'm taking all the risk, because the location isn't prime real estate at the moment. So...under the circumstances, I think I'm offering you a great deal."

Shelby nodded, but her eyes glazed over, and Ramos knew she was listening to his thoughts.

A few minutes later, Manetto stood and ended the meeting. "Thanks for coming, King. After I talk it over with Shelby, I'll let you know what I decide to do."

"Oh...sure." King said, standing. His confused gaze that he'd been dismissed so quickly came to rest on Shelby. "Uh...it was nice to meet you, Shelby. I hope you'll advise Mr. Manetto to take the deal. He won't find a better one for that piece of land."

"I'll be in touch," Manetto said, dismissing him before Shelby could say anything.

Ramos opened the door and ushered King out, then came back inside and sat down, eager to hear Shelby's take on the situation.

"Okay, Shelby, what did you get?" Manetto asked.

"Well, first off, I think King has an inside track to a development. From what I could gather, I think it has something to do with a metro station." She shook her head and let out a breath. "It's a little confusing, but I did see a picture in his head that looked like a drawing of a bunch of buildings next to some tracks."

"Like a mixed-use development?" Manetto asked. "A lot of times, when they put in a new metro line, they look around for adjoining property to build apartments or condos, and stores for shopping, that sort of thing. Is that what you saw?"

"You know, that might be it," Shelby agreed. "King has been buying up all the property in that area, so it makes sense."

Manetto smiled. "Did you pick up anything about who gave him this information?"

"He kept thinking about his partner at the transit authority, so it must have come from there. I only got a first name, Richard, but it sounds like they do this sort of thing a lot. I think Richard works for the transit authority, so he has the inside track about where they're going to put stops on the metro line. He passes that on to King, who can then buy up all the property before it becomes public knowledge. Oh...and I caught that they were silent partners, whatever that means."

"That's good information. Has he already bought the adjacent properties?"

"Yes, I think so. But he wants yours the most, because it's the biggest piece of land. It's also the key to his success in selling the whole package to investors to develop the area."

Manetto let out his breath, then a satisfied smile tilted his lips. "It's nice to have the inside scoop. I can definitely work with that. Thanks, Shelby. See? You are a financial advisor. One of the best. Am I right?"

Shelby smiled and shrugged her shoulders. "If you say so."

Manetto nodded. "Then I guess that's all for today. Thanks for coming in."

"You bet." Shelby stood. The smile stayed on her face, and Ramos could tell that she had enjoyed using her talents. She caught his gaze and nodded. "I do enjoy it, mostly because that guy was trying to pull something over on us."

"True," Ramos agreed. He wasn't about to point out that Manetto wasn't much different and ruin her sense of fairness. She must have heard that from his mind though, because her widened gaze caught his, and her lips twisted into a pout, but she just shook her head and stood.

Manetto thanked her again, and Ramos opened the door. He walked her down the hall to make sure King wasn't sticking around to ambush her. With the coast clear, he turned to her. "See...that wasn't so bad."

"You're right. I guess I shouldn't be so nervous about working for Uncle Joey. I mean...most of the time nothing bad happens, so I should remember those times instead of all the other times."

"Exactly," Ramos agreed. "And he's not so bad for a mob-boss."

Shelby nodded, but he didn't think she was convinced of that fact. Maybe someday she'd realize that, of all the mob-bosses, Manetto was probably one of the better ones to work for. At least Manetto wasn't as ruthless as most. And he didn't kill a lot of people. "Bye Shelby."

She chuckled. "Bye." As the elevator doors slid shut, she sent him an appreciative smile.

He hurried back to Manetto's office and took a seat in front of his desk. "That went well."

"Yes it did," Manetto said, a satisfied smile on his face. "We need to find out exactly who King's partner is. But that shouldn't be too hard now that we know his name is Richard and that he works for the transit authority. This is good."

"Want me to get started on that?" Ramos asked.

"Yes I do. Once we know more, we can meet with King again and make him a proposition he can't refuse. I'm pretty certain that what he's doing is illegal, but I'll check with my property attorney just to make sure."

Ramos got to work, spending the rest of the day looking into King's dealings and making a few phone calls. At the end of the day, he had the partner's full name and all the pertinent details. He joined Manetto in his office.

"This is the guy," Ramos said. "I'm sure you'll recognize the name now. He's that real estate developer who got appointed to the transit authority by the state legislature. It all looks pretty dirty to me."

"I think you're right. It's also enough information for me to ask for more money, or even get in on the development. What do you think I should do? Develop or sell?"

Ramos shrugged. "It depends on how involved you want to be with these guys. Developing the property might make you a lot more money in the long run. But if he already has investors, it might be easier to just ask for more money now."

"That's true," Manetto agreed. "I'm already up to my neck in the Riverside Plaza Development and that new grocery store next to it. I think I'll just go for the money."

"Makes sense to me."

"I'll have Jackie set up a meeting with King for tomorrow morning."

"Do you want Shelby to come?" Ramos asked.

"Hmm. Maybe not this time. There's not much more she can tell us that we don't already know, and I hate for her to see too much of my bad side."

Ramos chuckled and shook his head. "All right. See you tomorrow."

The next day, Ramos looked forward to their meeting with King. Trying to pull one over on Manetto was never a good idea, and putting him in his place would be sweet revenge. King showed up looking hopeful that he could make the deal.

Ramos almost wished Shelby was there, just to know how badly King wanted Manetto's property so they could get more money out of him, but he had to agree that Manetto had a point about keeping the worst side of their business from her. She already had plenty of misgivings about working for Manetto without knowing all the details.

"Thanks for inviting me back," King began, sitting down. "Are you ready to sell?"

"Yes, I think I am," Manetto answered. "But I've come across some information that's a little disturbing. Maybe you can clear it up?"

"Uh, sure," King said. His enthusiasm turned to wariness, and he sat up straighter in his chair.

"Good. Then I won't beat around the bush. I've found out that you have a silent partner who just so happens to work for the transit authority. It looks like he has the inside track to assigning metro stops in specific areas where you're buying up the properties. That could make both of you a lot of money."

King's eyes widened and his mouth dropped open.

"As I'm sure you know, there is some concern about the legality of your whole set-up. So here's what I'm going to do. Since my property is central to your plans, you can either pay me what I think it's worth, or I can call a certain nosy reporter and tell her my suspicions. Anonymously of course. I don't imagine your silent partner would be thrilled to know he's been found out. Just think...you could both end up in jail."

"What? How did you...this is insane. There's no connection between the two of us. There's no way you could prove any of it."

"I think you might be mistaken," Manetto replied. "I have resources in places you don't even know about. Do you really want to take me on?"

King swallowed and let out his breath. "All right. What do you propose?"

"I'm willing to sell you the property, but at a higher cost."

"How much?" he asked.

Manetto's lips turned up into a predatory smile, reminding Ramos of a wolf or lion playing with his food before going in for the kill. "How much do you think it's worth?"

King frowned and pursed his lips. He didn't seem to like being put on the spot. Ramos watched him closely. He'd been studying King just like he would if they were playing poker. It was something he'd always been good at and, from

King's expression, he was pretty sure he'd know if he was bluffing.

"All right," King said. "We can go five million, and that's being generous."

Manetto glanced at Ramos. He shook his head.

"You disappoint me," Manetto said. "I'm not unreasonable, but if you wish to continue your scheme in the future, I need more than that."

King huffed out a breath. "But we need to make some money on this deal. You have to give me that."

"Make money? I think you'll do well to break even, especially if you want to stay out of jail. I would think your freedom would be worth a few million more."

King squirmed in his seat. But in the end, he admitted defeat. "How much do you want?"

Manetto smiled, knowing he had him right where he wanted him. "I think ten million will do."

"Ten! But that's too high. We'll barely make that amount."

Manetto shrugged. "It's up to you. Take it or leave it. It's all the same to me."

Ultimately, King left with an agreement to pay Manetto ten million for the property. He had figured out that the exorbitant price included hush money for the project. That was a little hard for him to understand but, in the end, it finally got through to him.

"Do you think he'll cause any problems?" Manetto asked Ramos.

"Him? No. He's all bluster and no bite. I can't say the same for his partner, but it might keep them honest in the future."

Manetto chuckled. "True enough."

Manetto's phone rang and he picked it up. He spoke for a few minutes. From what he said, Ramos knew something had come up that wasn't good. He hung up and glanced at Ramos.

"That was Bruno in Orlando. Zack stopped by yesterday like he was supposed to, but Bruno thought he wasn't as forthcoming as he should be. He called to tell me that I should keep an eye on Zack, because he might be scheming something of his own. Zack should arrive in Miami tonight to meet with Saunders tomorrow morning. I might need to send you down there to check up on him and find out what's going on."

Ramos's gaze narrowed. Zack was the mastermind behind the bomb that blew up the Passinis' yacht. Zack had hoped to kill both Ramos and Manetto and blame it on the Passinis. With Shelby's help, they'd figured it out and confronted Zack.

He'd confessed to the whole thing but, instead of killing him for it, Manetto had decided to put him to work as a courier. It was a dangerous job, but better than being dead. Still, Ramos wasn't sure Zack could be trusted. "Of course. I'll get a bag packed."

"Good. Don't be too rough on the kid. He's not familiar with how I do things, so that could be all it is."

"I won't. But what about Bruno? Are you sure you can trust him?"

Manetto's brows rose, then he nodded his head. "I suppose that's a concern. Bruno is new, but I don't think he'd want to jeopardize our relationship, or his reputation, at this point."

Ramos nodded. Bruno had taken over Carson's empire after Ramos had taken Carson out. The organization had needed a complete overhaul, and Bruno had been more than pleased to keep the business going with Manetto, so it didn't make sense that he'd try to sabotage it now. "I'll find out what's going on and let you know."

"Good. I'll make the arrangements. The jet should be ready to go in about an hour."

Ramos didn't waste any time getting ready. He was used to these overnight excursions, and already had a carry-on bag packed with essentials. He only needed to add a few clothes for the trip. Within an hour, he had boarded the plane and was in the air.

At the Miami airport, he rented a car, remembering the last time he'd been there with Shelby. His brother, Javier, lived in the city, but he thought Ramos was dead. As much as Ramos would like to change that, he knew it wasn't a good idea. Having a family could be used against him. It was a liability that could get Javier killed, and he wasn't about to put his brother in danger.

It reminded him of the information that Sloan had given him about his father. He'd tried to put it from his mind, but what if his father was alive? The odds against that were almost one hundred percent. But with Cuba only a hundred miles away from here, he wondered if he should call Sloan and see if she'd found out any more about him. Maybe he could take an extra day or two and visit Cuba?

Ramos drove to South Beach and turned down Ocean Drive. The sun had set, and dusk turned the sky gray, but here on Ocean Drive, all the lights kept it bright and vibrant with plenty to see and do. Zack's itinerary called for him to stay at the Park Hotel for the night, so that's where Ramos headed.

He registered for a room, and it didn't take long to settle in. Zack would probably arrive in the next couple of hours, and Ramos hoped to catch sight of him when he did. He headed down to the bar and found a small table close to the doors where he could keep watch.

After an hour, his vigilance payed off as Zack entered the hotel pulling a small luggage carrier. He held onto the handle of a briefcase with his other hand. Ramos followed him at a distance, then waited for Zack to get on the elevator. Just before the doors closed, Ramos ducked inside.

Zack jerked back with alarm, and he sucked in a surprised breath. "Ra..Ramos. What are you doing here?"

Ramos smiled and casually leaned against the side of the elevator. "What do you think? Manetto sent me to check up on you."

"What? Why? I haven't done anything wrong."

Ramos narrowed his gaze. "Is that right?"

"Yes. I would never cross Manetto. You know that."

"Actually, I don't. But Manetto thinks you're worth saving, so that's why you're not dead. I hope you're worth it."

The elevator doors opened, and Ramos followed Zack onto the sixth floor. "I have everything," Zack said. "And I've been following the itinerary. So I don't understand why you're here." Letting go of his luggage, he put the key card in the lock and opened the door.

"Let me get that for you." Ramos grabbed Zack's luggage and followed him inside. After Zack secured the door with the lock and chain, he tossed the briefcase and keys on the bed.

"So what's going on?" Zack asked.

"Manetto got a call from Bruno this morning. Bruno claimed that you might have something of your own going down, and he wanted Manetto to know about it."

Zack's mouth turned down. "What? Did he say why he thought that?"

Ramos shook his head. "Not that Manetto told me." At Zack's frustrated growl, Ramos continued. "Why would Bruno get that impression?"

Zack let out a breath, and brushed his hand through his hair. "I don't know, but if you ask me, I think Bruno is the one with something to hide. He kept asking me questions about the diamonds, and it made me nervous. He's not supposed to know my itinerary, is he?"

Zack had a point. "You're right. He's not. Maybe he's just protecting Manetto's business interests, since you're the new guy."

"Maybe. But that's not the vibe I got."

"Let's say you're right. What does he have to gain?"

Zack shrugged. "He could take me out and keep the diamonds. Then he could just tell Manetto that I flew the coop, and he shouldn't have trusted me."

"Hang on," Ramos said. "Be careful who you badmouth, you never know when it might come back to bite you."

Zack blew out a breath and threw himself into a chair by the desk. He mumbled something, and Ramos was pretty sure what it was. "You think I'm too set in my ways to consider it?"

Zack's startled gaze flew to Ramos, and he quickly shook his head in denial. "No, not at all. But since I'm the new guy, it makes sense that you'd trust him over me."

Ramos decided to cut him some slack. "You're right. Why don't you show me what you've got so far?"

Zack nodded, then stood and unlocked the briefcase with a special code. He opened a hidden compartment in the bottom of the case and pulled it away. Tucked inside was a long, thin, black leather box, which he pulled out and handed to Ramos.

"The first batch is all there, you can see that for yourself."

Ramos set the box on the round coffee table and carefully opened the lid. A plastic bag with close to twenty diamonds filled the inside. He pulled one of the diamonds out of the bag to examine it. "Hand me your eyepiece."

Zack took it out of his briefcase and handed it over. Ramos held the diamond to the light and inspected it through the eyepiece. He found what he was looking for and nodded. "This one looks good. Tell me exactly what Bruno said that made you suspicious."

"After the trade, he asked me where I was headed next. I didn't think that was something he should know, so I told him it was none of his business. It probably ticked him off, because he told me to watch whose toes I stepped on, or I wouldn't have any left." Zack shrugged. "I guess we didn't leave on the best of terms, but he was the one who was out of line."

Ramos nodded. "And you checked all of the diamonds after that? To make sure he didn't cheat you?"

"Yes," Zack said, pleased that Ramos understood what he'd been saying. "They were all there, so I decided to leave early this morning, before he had a chance to jump me. I had no idea that he'd called Manetto about it."

Ramos could hardly believe that Bruno would double-cross Manetto, but stranger things had happened. "So you didn't tell him you were headed to Miami?"

"No."

Ramos couldn't remember if Manetto had mentioned it to Bruno over the phone, but it was a possiblity. "Do you know if anyone followed you here?"

"I don't think so." Zack shrugged. "But what do I know? I'm just a lowly courier."

Ramos smiled. He believed Zack. "I'll bet Bruno never thought that Manetto would send me so quickly. So if he's planning to take you out, we'll find out soon enough."

"What does that mean?"

"Don't worry. He doesn't know I'm here, so I think we should go ahead with your visit to Saunders' store tomorrow. You can pick up the merchandise, and I'll catch whoever's after you."

Zack sniffed and shook his head. "Fine. But after this, I want a different job."

"All you have to do is prove yourself to Manetto. He always rewards loyalty. He's also impressed by people who take the initiative and figure things out on their own. If you remember, that's why he let you live, so don't screw this up."

This time Zack nodded with more enthusiasm. "I can do that. I want to prove myself."

"Good." Ramos checked his watch. It was close to seven, and he was tempted to go out on the town, but it would be bad if someone from Bruno's organization spotted him. Still, it wouldn't hurt to drive somewhere else for dinner. "You want to head to Little Havana for some Cuban food?"

Zack's eyes widened with surprise. "Sure. I've never had Cuban food before."

"Okay. Let's go."

Ramos made sure they weren't followed to the parking garage, where they got in his car and drove onto the street. He kept watch in his rearview mirror, but couldn't see a sign of anyone on his tail. Taking the next street, he turned toward Little Havana and drove in a round-about way, just in case.

Ramos had last visited Little Havana a couple of months ago after Carson's death. Manetto had sent him to Miami to establish the connection with Saunders. Ramos knew he'd visited Little Havana as a kid when he was around eight years old, but he was too young to remember much.

But he'd remembered the food, because his mother had made it during his childhood. Still, it wasn't until now that he wanted to embrace his past. When he'd been in Miami with Shelby, he'd never thought of taking her there, but that was because he'd been wrapped up in the news that his brother was alive and well. Now...there was a small hope in his heart of finding his father. If that happened, then maybe he could risk letting Javier into his life.

With a sudden craving for a 'frita,' a Cuban beef and pork burger topped with shoestring potatoes on Cuban bread, he drove to the famous El Rey de las Fritas. The crowd wasn't too bad, and after they were seated, the waiter took their orders.

While waiting for their food, Ramos asked Zack how things had been going, and Zack opened up a little. Ramos could see the ambition in him, and he hoped Zack used it wisely.

Their food arrived, and they spent the next few minutes satisfying their hunger. Then Ramos asked Zack what the plan was for the next day.

"I'm meeting Saunders at nine a.m. at his jewelry store. I guess if someone's watching me, they'll be waiting until I come out. At least that's what I'd do."

"I agree. If that happens, I want to have a plan in place, but first, I need to call Manetto, and let him know what's going on. He might have something to add. I'll call him when we get back to the hotel. Then we can figure this out."

Mentioning Manetto and the whole deal must have put a damper on Zack's appetite, because he barely touched his food after that. Since they were basically done, they left the restaurant and headed back to the hotel, where they went their separate ways. "I'll come to your room after I talk to Manetto," Ramos said.

Back in his room, Ramos put the call through and explained what he'd found out from Zack. "I believe him, so I think I should shadow Zack tomorrow and see if anyone is following him."

"That's a good idea," Manetto agreed. "And I'm going to give Bruno a courtesy call and tell him that I'm concerned about his organization. After we chat, I'll let you know what I think, and we can plan accordingly."

"Sounds good."

A few minutes later, Manetto called him back. "Bruno swears that he has nothing planned so, if he did, I'm sure he'll cancel it now. Maybe I shouldn't have tipped him off, but sometimes that's the best way to keep my so-called friends in check. Watch out for Zack, and take care of anyone who shows up. If you need help, give our friend, Charlie, a call. He owes me a favor, and I'm sure he'd help with whatever you need."

Charlie was their removal contact in Miami. He was dependable when it came to disposing of bodies and cleaning up the mess if Ramos ended up killing someone. "Will do. I'll let you know what happens."

Ramos took the elevator to Zack's floor and knocked on his door. Zack let Ramos in, and they began to figure out their moves for the next day. After discussing all of their options and coming up with a decent plan, Ramos was ready to call it a night.

"See you in the morning," he said, then made his way back to his room and got ready for bed. Before turning out the light, he pulled the card with Sloan's name and number from his wallet. On impulse, he pushed in the numbers and waited.

"Hello?"

"Sloan. It's Ramos."

Silence answered him, then she spoke a little breathlessly. "Ramos...what a surprise. Uh...how are you?"

"Good." He let out a breath, then took the plunge. "I'm actually in Miami right now, and I was wondering if you found out anything more about my father."

"What? You're in Miami? That's crazy. I'm actually here...in Cuba. Hey...do you want to come? I'm here on an assignment, but I should have some spare time to help you find out more about your dad."

Ramos could hardly believe it. This was a chance he couldn't pass up. "Yeah. I think I can swing it. I should be done with my business here sometime tomorrow. I could catch a flight the next day. What do I need to do to be allowed into the country?"

"Um...since I just went through all of that, I can send a fax to your hotel in the morning with all of the information that you'll need to board the plane. If you want, I could make your reservation for you. I think there's a flight that leaves for Cuba at the same time every afternoon, so that shouldn't be a problem. You have your passport, right?"

"Yeah."

"Good. Then I'll get it all worked out and call you tomorrow."

"Okay," he agreed, surprised at how fast she had taken charge. He gave her the name and address of his hotel, then added, "I can get my own ticket."

"Oh, don't worry about it. It's the least I can do. Besides, I'm excited to see you again." He was slow to answer, so she spoke into the silence. "Uh...so...check everything over, and let me know if you have any questions."

"Sure. Thanks Sloan." He disconnected and let out a breath, wondering what he'd just gotten himself into. He'd never expected her to be there and thought it would take more time to get everything worked out.

He didn't even know why she was there in the first place. She called it an assignment, but what did that entail? With a spy like Sloan, anything could happen.

It also bothered him that she hadn't followed through with his request to take him with her the next time she was there. Still, he had to believe she'd told him the truth about his father. If going to Cuba was the only way to find out what had happened to him, he had to go.

He just hoped she wasn't keeping secrets from him like last time.

Chapter 8

The next morning, Ramos followed Zack to Saunders' store. Since the store was only a block away from the hotel, Zack walked the distance, playing his part well by never once looking over his shoulder. The briefcase was designed with a chain that attached to his wrist in case anyone tried to steal it from him. Ramos kept a discreet watch but detected nothing from the people around him.

With the protocols Saunders had set up for his high-end jewelry store, Ramos knew Zack was safe once he entered the building, so he found a place to observe from across the street and settled in to watch. Half an hour later, Zack came out.

Zack hesitated on the sidewalk, looking in both directions, then turned the opposite way from which he'd come. Was he giving Ramos the slip? That's when Ramos noticed the man jay-walking across the street ahead of him. He was in a hurry, and closing in on Zack.

Ramos calculated the distance and kept on his side of the street, keeping up with the man. All at once, Zack darted into traffic. Ramos sucked in his breath as Zack narrowly missed getting hit by an oncoming car. Once he'd made it across both lanes, Ramos could breathe again.

Knowing he'd been made, the man hurried to catch up to him, but Zack kept to the plan and ran in Ramos's direction, leading his pursuer straight toward Ramos. The man was so intent on Zack that he didn't even notice Ramos until Ramos stepped into his path. Their gazes met, and surprised shock stopped Ramos in his tracks. Esposito was a crooked cop, and they'd met once before when Esposito had been working for Carson.

Esposito's eyes widened as well. He gasped and then turned to run, but not before Ramos grabbed his wrist and pulled his arm behind him. Ramos used Esposito's momentum to carry them through the doors of a small bistro, pushing him through the crowded tables and into the kitchen.

"Police business," he announced to the startled workers. Then he asked one of the cooks where the back entrance was and followed the man's directions until coming out into an alley. He shoved Esposito to the ground and pulled out his gun. Esposito scrambled to a sitting position against the brick wall and held up his hands.

"Wait! Don't shoot. This wasn't my idea. I'll tell you who ordered it."

Ramos held the gun steady, letting him sweat for a minute, before slightly lowering it. "I'm listening."

"It was Bruno. He told me to get the briefcase. I don't even know what's in it. But I had to do it. He was threatening to get me fired from my job with the police."

"Bruno, huh? You're saying that Bruno is double-crossing Manetto?"

Esposito's gaze darted around the alley, sensing a trap. "Yeah."

"Hmm...that's not what he said."

Esposito's eyes bulged, and his face paled. "Okay...okay. It wasn't him, but someone in his organization. You gotta believe me."

"That's a problem," Ramos answered. "You're not as convincing as you think." He raised his gun, and Esposito held his arms in front of him like a shield.

"Wait. I can give you his name."

Ramos lowered his gun and let out a breath. Now Esposito was talking. "What is it?"

"Uh...you won't kill me, right?"

Ramos holstered his gun. "Not yet. Now talk."

"It's Garland...Seth Garland. He's Bruno's brother-in-law. He knew about the diamonds and sent me after them."

Ramos watched Esposito's face to determine if he was telling the truth. "All right. I'll buy it. But it still doesn't answer why Bruno was suspicious of Zack in the first place."

"I don't know anything about that."

From the desperation in his voice, Ramos believed him. Now it was time to decide whether to turn Esposito into a corpse, or use him as a witness against Seth to help out Bruno. As long as Bruno hadn't planned the whole thing with Seth, that might be the best plan, but he'd let Manetto decide how to proceed.

Just then, a car pulled up to the alley entrance, and Zack jumped out. Ramos grabbed Esposito, twisting him so his face was against the wall, and pulled his hands behind his back. Zack handed him a zip tie, and Ramos pulled it tight around Esposito's wrists.

"I think Bruno might want to have a talk with you," Ramos said. He hustled Esposito to the car and shoved him into the back seat, then sat beside him.

Zack got back into the driver's seat and started the car. "Where to?" he asked.

"Let's find a private place to talk."

Esposito stiffened beside him, and Ramos knew Esposito thought that Ramos was telling Zack to find a private place to kill him. It didn't bother Ramos in the least. Not after what Esposito had put Shelby through in Orlando. Besides, it could still happen.

Several minutes later, Zack pulled off the road and down a street that ran beside a wildlife refuge. Ramos smiled at the irony that Zack thought he'd meant a good place to dump a body too, since throwing him into the gator-infested waters would do the trick.

Zack pulled into a turn-out and parked the car. He jumped out of the front seat and opened Esposito's door. Ramos got out as well and walked around the car to Zack's side. "Watch him, but don't kill him yet, I need to talk to Manetto."

Zack nodded and pulled out his Glock. Ramos shook his head at Zack's enthusiasm, then pulled out his phone and walked away from the car for some privacy.

"I caught the guy," Ramos began. "His name's Esposito. He said he wasn't going after Zack for Bruno, but for Bruno's brother-in-law. A guy named Seth Garland."

"Hmm...that doesn't bode well for Bruno's organization, unless they're in on it together."

"True. But if they're not, it might be a gesture of good will to let Bruno deal with it."

"You're right. It would also give me an edge in my dealings with Bruno. If he makes excuses and doesn't take care of the problem, then I'll know he was in on it. If he wasn't in on it, he'll thank me for uncovering the double-crosser, and owe me a favor." Manetto sighed. "All right. I'll put a call through to Bruno and call you back."

Ramos disconnected and paced back and forth along the road. For the beginning of March, it was a warm, sunny day. Once he got this straightened out, he might even be heading to Cuba tomorrow. A sudden memory came to him of a woman saying that Cuba was an island paradise. He'd only thought of it as a place to get away from. Maybe it was a little of both.

His phone rang, and he quickly answered. "Bruno sounded appalled," Manetto began. "So I don't think he was in on it, but he wants to take care of the problem himself. He said this Esposito fellow is a leftover from Carson's days, and he's a cop."

"That's true," Ramos agreed. "I met him when I was there with Shelby. I told Detective Fitch that he was working for Carson, so I'm a little surprised he's still around."

"Well, I doubt he will be for long. But you were right; Bruno wants to talk with him. He has a man there in Miami who will take Esposito off your hands. Here's the address where you're to meet him." Manetto gave Ramos the name and address, then disconnected with instructions to call when the job was done.

Ramos got back to the car and smiled at Esposito. "Good news. It looks like you're going to live a little longer." Esposito sagged with relief. Ramos turned to Zack and told him where to drive next, and they were soon on the road to meet Bruno's man.

They pulled into a run-down neighborhood with only a few houses that looked habitable. Outside the last house on the street, a man straightened from his perch on the porch and waited for them to stop. From what Ramos could see, he wasn't holding a gun but, in this business, that didn't mean he wasn't dangerous.

"Wait here," Ramos told Zack. "And keep the car running."

Since Ramos wasn't sure of this guy, he wanted to keep his options open. He opened Esposito's door and helped him out, then stood behind him with his gun drawn. "He's all yours," Ramos said. The man grunted and grabbed Esposito's arm.

As they walked into the house, Ramos got back in the car and told Zack to take them back to the hotel. He let out a breath, grateful to let someone else take care of Esposito. Zack pulled into the parking lot, and they both got out of the car.

"What's next for you?" Ramos asked him.

"I've got two more stops to make before I work out the deal with our buyers."

"Manetto wants you to do the deal? I'm impressed."

Zack smiled. "Well, I'm hoping to prove my worth."

"That should do it." Ramos hoped Zack came through, or he wasn't going to last long. "Are you headed out today?"

"Yes. I need to be on the road by two o'clock, or I'll miss my next appointment."

Ramos checked his watch. It was already after one. "I'll leave you to it."

"Thanks for your help. I appreciate it."

"No problem."

After shaking hands, they entered the hotel and went their separate ways. Ramos checked with the front desk to see if Sloan had sent him anything. Sure enough, a stack of papers with travel information and his plane ticket awaited him. The flight left the next afternoon and landed in Havana less than an hour later.

He took everything up to his room and called Manetto. "Everything's taken care of."

"Good. How's Zack doing?"

"I think he'll be fine. I didn't know you were letting him make the deal, though."

"I know," Manetto agreed. "I'm not so sure that was a good idea on my part, but you've got to admit, the kid has a lot of ambition."

"That's true. As long as you can trust him."

"Yes...but without giving someone a chance, how do you know? Anyway...I thought maybe you could keep an eye on him for me. His next appointment isn't for a few days, but I think we can let him handle that one.

"It's the last appointment here at home that I'm concerned about. It's a few weeks from now, but I'd like you to shadow him while he sets it up. After that, he'll be making the deal, and I want him to finish everything up on his own. What do you think?"

"From what I've observed, I think he'll do great." Ramos took a deep breath and let it out. "There is something that's come up. So, if you can spare me, I could use the next few days off."

"Is it your brother? He's there in Miami, isn't he?"

"Yes, but I'm not ready to involve him in my life. It's something else."

Ramos hadn't told Manetto about Sloan's information that his father could still be alive, and he wasn't sure he wanted to. "While I'm this close, I thought I'd take a detour to Cuba. Just to get some closure. You know that's where I'm from. With my parents dead, and no real memories of my family, I thought it might...be nice."

"Do you have relatives there?"

"I honestly don't know."

"Hmm. You're not planning to leave the business, are you?" Manetto asked.

"No. I wouldn't think of it. Whatever I find, nothing will change."

"Fine. Take all the time you need. I'd tell you to take the jet, but I don't think my pilots have clearance to fly into Cuba."

Ramos smiled and shook his head. "Don't worry about it. There's a daily flight from here, so it's easy to get a ticket. In fact..." Ramos hesitated, but he knew he needed to be honest with Manetto, and tell him the truth.

"There's something you need to know," Ramos began. "One day, not long after my family arrived in the states, my father went to work and never came home. We never knew what happened to him, and it broke my mother's heart.

"The last time I spoke to Sloan, she had some information about him. She told me that she found out he was taken back to Cuba against his will, and that he might still be alive. That's the real reason I want to go."

"Holy hell," Manetto said. "You know I like to stay out of your personal business, but this...why didn't you tell me?"

"I guess because my past is not something I've wanted to think about...or revisit. But now...I don't think he's alive, but it would be nice to know for sure."

"I can see that," Manetto said. "What about Sloan? Have you told her you're going?"

"That's the thing. I called her last night. She's there right now, and she's already made arrangements for me to fly down and meet her there tomorrow. I was a bit surprised at how fast she managed it, but that doesn't change the fact that I need to go. So I don't really need the jet, since she's already arranged a plane ticket for me."

Manetto grunted. "You know how I feel about Sloan. You can't trust her. Are you sure you want to do this?"

"Yes. I'll be fine."

Manetto let out a breath. "I'm sure you will. Just be careful." He paused before continuing, "And since you're going to be there, why don't you bring me back some of those famous Cuban cigars?"

"Sure. I'll do it."

"And Ramos," he said. "I hope you find him."

They disconnected, and Ramos let out a breath. Now that he was actually going, he hoped he'd made the right decision. He checked the papers Sloan had left him, going over the mandated questionnaire she'd sent. Most of it was blank for him to fill out, but she'd put a check mark in the box that stated his reason for going to Cuba was to visit family.

At least she hadn't used his family name. If his father had left because of political reasons, Ramos didn't want the connection between them known. Of course, how else was he supposed to find out what had happened to him? Maybe the name, Ramirez, was common enough that he didn't have to worry about it.

After filling everything out, he put a call through to Sloan. "The paperwork's done."

"Great," she said. "You'll need to have proof of a hotel reservation as well. I thought you could stay at the same hotel as me, but I'll let you make the reservation. You should do it today so you can show the customs agent."

Ramos wrote down the name of the hotel and the other things she told him he'd need for his visit.

"One more thing," Sloan said. "They're pretty picky about what you bring through customs, so you'll have to leave your gun at home."

"I'm sure I can manage," he quipped. "Anything else?"

"No. I'll be waiting to pick you up at the airport, so I'll see you tomorrow."

They said their goodbyes and disconnected. Ramos quickly made a reservation at the hotel for two nights. Once that was done, he settled back into his chair and let out a breath. A sliver of unease ran down his spine. Would Sloan tell him the real reason for her visit to Cuba?

Maybe the reason she was there didn't really matter. He certainly wasn't going to get mixed up in her schemes this time, so it wasn't something he should worry about.

He let out a sigh and shook his head. That was easier said than done, and he couldn't shake the feeling that getting involved with Sloan could turn into something like Mexico. Only this time it was worse, because he had no idea what he was walking into.

Chapter 9

The plane landed at the Havana airport. Ramos carried a medium-sized duffel bag over his shoulder, which contained a few clothes and other accessories that he might need for the trip. For a small fee, he'd left everything else at the hotel in Miami.

Wearing a basic white t-shirt and jeans, he headed toward the service area and waited to go through customs. Thanks to Sloan, he had everything he needed, and he breezed through customs without a problem. It also helped that he spoke Spanish, and carried only one bag.

He walked through the airport and followed the signs to the pick-up zone. He'd sent a text to Sloan, and she'd told him she was already there, and to look for a red convertible.

Glancing at the cars, it wasn't hard to spot her, and a big smile broke out on his face. She drove an old, nineteen-fifty era, Buick convertible. She waved at him, and he hurried to the car. "Nice," he said, throwing his duffel bag into the back. He slipped into the passenger seat and closed the door.

Sloan smiled, but shook her head and let out a dramatic sigh.

"What?"

She shrugged. "It's just what I thought." She caught his gaze. "You were more excited to see the car than you were to see me."

Ramos chuckled. "Isn't that why you drove it?"

Her lips turned into a pouty frown, and she shrugged. "Maybe." She turned her head to glance at the road before pulling onto the street, and Ramos had to admit that she was the real reason the car looked so hot. She'd tied her glossy, dark hair back with a yellow scarf, and the warmth of her smile could melt the coldest heart.

Not wanting that to happen to him again, he turned his focus to his surroundings. The weather was the perfect blend of warmth combined with soft Caribbean breezes. The area around the airport looked much like any industrial zone, and they soon turned onto the freeway to head toward the city.

"We'll take the scenic route into Old Havana so you can see the sights," Sloan said. "We'll drive through the famous Malecón to get there. It's a broad seawall that stretches about eight miles across the harbor and into Old Havana. Our hotel is just on the other side."

Ramos drank in the sights and sounds of the island, but it wasn't until they reached the Malecón that he could smell the sea. Looking out into the ocean, he marveled at the bright blue colors. As they got closer to the old town, the buildings became more colorful, with spots of red, blue, lime green and yellow. It was a feast for the eyes, with cars punctuating the streets and sporting similar colors.

Sloan pulled off the Malecón and into Old Havana. Along the streets here, most of the buildings had columns at the bottom with ornate ironwork along the balconies on top. She pulled in front of their hotel and parked.

This hotel was situated on the street corner and followed the curve of the street with columns around the bottom and rising to four stories in height. It was painted white with a bright blue trim around the windows and doorways. With a smile, Ramos grabbed his duffel bag and followed Sloan inside.

The beautiful lobby was filled with arches and columns. It sported a tile floor, and track lighting shone down from the high vaulted ceiling. It was tastefully decorated with pedestal statues, leather couches, and glass tables topped with beautiful flower arrangements. Ramos shook his head. This wasn't at all what he'd pictured Cuba to look like.

At the desk, Ramos dropped his bag to the floor, and successfully checked into his room. He spoke in Spanish, grateful it was good enough to be easily understood, although he was certain everyone spoke English as well. After getting his key, Sloan led him to the elevators.

"I think you'll love the rooms. What floor are you on?" she asked, pushing the elevator call button.

"Three." He glanced her way, surprised that she hadn't tried to talk him into sharing a room with her. "Where are you?"

"I'm on four."

He raised his brows and caught her gaze. She glanced away with a guilty flush, and his senses went on full alert. "What else is going on?"

"Well...the thing is...I'm not exactly here alone. You remember? After Mexico they gave me a partner?" At Ramos's nod, she continued. "Well, he's here too."

"Oh." Ramos hadn't expected that.

"It's not like that," she quickly explained. "We're not...we're in different rooms. It's totally professional."

"Right."

She shook her head. "It's just...well...he's not real happy you're here, but he'll just have to get over it."

"I see." The elevator doors opened, and they stepped inside. "Actually, I'm a bit surprised that you're not staying at the American Embassy."

Sloan's brows rose, and she shook her head. "Uh...nope."

"So why are you here?"

Before she could explain, the elevator doors opened, and they stepped onto the third floor. Glancing both ways, and finding another couple in the hall, she whispered, "I'll tell you in your room."

He nodded and turned down the hall. Finding the right door, he put in the key card and pushed it open. Inside, the room opened to a sitting room on one side with a couch and small television, with the bedroom and bathroom on the other side.

Although it was beautifully done, it held the musty odor of an old building. He threw his bag onto the bed and pulled the curtains aside, wanting some fresh air. Pulling the windows open, he enjoyed the view below of cobblestone streets, and the fresh, ocean breeze.

"It's nice." He turned back to Sloan and gestured toward the couch. "So, what's going on?" They sat down, and he waited for her to explain.

"Well, my official reason for being here is to visit relatives. Kind of like you. I don't really have any relatives in Cuba, but it's a good cover. My real assignment is a little more complicated than that. I'm actually looking for the people responsible for the attacks on the American Embassy."

"There was an attack?"

"Yes, but it wasn't the usual attack with guns or anything like that. And I can tell you about it, because it's been in the news. Our people in the embassy have reported several health problems, mostly to do with hearing loss and headaches.

"We can only surmise that they're under attack by something like a sonic device. The Cuban government isn't claiming responsibility and, in some ways, it makes sense. I mean, why would they do something like that? Why would anyone?"

"I don't think Cubans like Americans much, so who knows?" Ramos shrugged. "How are you supposed to find out what happened?"

"Oh, it's something we've been working on for the last week, and we've made some good progress. I have contacts here, but I'm probably not supposed to tell you that part."

"So, am I going to meet your partner?"

She let out a sigh. "Probably. I mean...he knows you're here, but he just thinks the timing is a coincidence...which, I guess it is, since he doesn't know what I told you about your father. I even think he'd like to meet you, so that makes it easier for him to accept that you're here."

"Why?"

"Well, you have a reputation after what happened in Mexico." At Ramos's raised brows, she continued. "Seriously! You're like a legend in the department." She shrugged. "Anyway..."

"Dammit, Sloan. A legend?" He was flattered, but he didn't want the attention. "I need to stay anonymous."

"I know and I'm sorry. But there wasn't much I could do about that. Anyway, depending on how our investigation goes, I should still have plenty of time to help you figure out what happened to your father."

Ramos nodded, grateful she hadn't asked for his help with this assignment and, if her partner was here, it also answered his question about why she hadn't invited him to come with her.

"Well, now that I'm here," he began. "You can tell me everything you know about my father, and why you think he was brought back against his will." She hesitated, so he continued, "And don't worry about getting my hopes up. I don't expect to find him alive after all this time."

"Okay, sure." She glanced at her hands and nervously clasped them together. "I don't know where to start, but the whole reason he was targeted was because he was working with the U.S. government."

"What?" A ripple of shock ran over Ramos. That was the last thing he'd expected her to say.

"I don't have a lot of details. All I know is that it happened in the nineties after the collapse of the Soviet Union and the horrible economic conditions it placed on the Cubans. It was bad enough that people were starving. Rafael was in the Cuban military, and he began to speak out against the Cuban government. He must have been somewhat successful, because he got the attention of some Cuban-Americans in the states, and they alerted our government.

"Apparently, we sent him funds to help his cause and bring down the regime. But the wrong people must have found out, and they tried to stop him. Luckily, he managed to get out of Cuba with your family before that happened. I guess he thought he was safe in the states, because he kept speaking out and making plans with some of the Cubans who'd immigrated with him.

"Sometime after that, their group was attacked, and Rafael was taken. One of the men witnessed his kidnapping and barely escaped with his life. He asked the U.S. government to intervene, but when our people inquired about the incident, the Cuban government denied any such thing, and there was nothing else they could do."

"Do you know who this man was?" Ramos asked.

"No. I'm afraid not. Why? Do you remember something?"

"I'm not sure, but I think I may have met him. In fact, it wasn't long after my father disappeared that a man came to see us. He arranged and paid for our move from Miami to Orlando. I'll bet anything that it was the same man."

Ramos didn't remember much about that time, but he did remember getting help from an older man whose face was a mask of bruises. "I think he came to see us in Orlando a couple of times after that, but then we never saw him again."

Sloan nodded. "I guess it could have been him."

Ramos didn't know if the man was still alive, but it would be nice to talk to him if he was. There was so much he could learn from him about his father. "How did you find out about all this?"

Sloan glanced away. "There was an opening for some covert assignments here in Cuba, and I applied. It was right up my alley because I'm Latino, and I speak fluent Spanish. It puts me in high demand for this sort of thing. Anyway, while I was prepping, I managed to get my hands on some files of the Cubans who had fled the country during that time."

Ramos glanced sharply at her, and he knew the only reason she'd gone to all that work was because he'd told her a little about his past. "But how did you connect the names? I never told you my real name was Ramirez."

She shrugged. "I may have looked you up in our database."

Ramos tensed. After he'd left Orlando, he'd hired an attorney to legally change his name. But he didn't know he could be found on a government database. "What do you mean?"

Sloan let out a breath and stood, pacing to the windows overlooking the square. "It's all there for anyone working in the government to see. You have a juvie record under Alejandro Ramirez. That's the file you found in my apartment, but it's sealed, so I don't know what happened to you, or why you left Orlando. But later on it shows that you legally changed your last name to Ramos."

He wasn't sure he believed her. "Is there more?"

"Not officially," she said, then turned to face him. "You may have been a person of interest in a few outstanding cases, but that doesn't mean you're guilty of anything."

"That's good to know." He wouldn't be surprised if he was flagged for possible criminal activity, and he sure as hell didn't want anyone taking a closer look. Of course, they had to have some intel on him since Sloan had involved him with her deal in Mexico. Did that mean they might try to build a case against him in the future? His stomach tightened. Why had he ever helped Sloan?

"Don't worry," Sloan said. "You earned some points for helping me in Mexico, so I don't think anyone will come after you...as long as you keep your nose clean."

As reassuring as she tried to make that sound, it didn't help much.

She came back to the couch and sat down. "Anyway, back to your father. After searching through the Cuban files, I happened upon one with the name 'Rafael Ramirez' on it. All of your family's names were listed there, along with the day you came through immigration and were granted asylum. That's when I put it together and told you about it at Christmas."

Ramos nodded and glanced at Sloan. There was nothing he could do about her involvement in his life now, so he might as well see where this went. "So, where do we go from here? How would I find out what happened to him?"

"Well, you're in luck. I have a copy of your father's file in my room. I brought it with me in case I had time to look into it while I was here. There are a few addresses in it, and I think one is an address of where you lived here in Havana. There's also another one for some relatives, possibly your grandparents. Who knows, maybe they're still there?"

Ramos found it hard to take a breath. He had grandparents that could still be alive? He'd spent most of his life alone. It was hard to believe he had family at all. When he'd found his brother, it had changed him, but this? Could he even hope they'd be there?

"I'll get it and be right back."

He barely heard her leave. Knowing he had relatives who might know what had happened to his father sent shock waves through him. Could his father be alive after all? If he'd been in prison, Ramos hated to think he was still there, but if he'd ever been released and gone looking for his family, he never would have found them. With his mother dead, and both he and his brother changing their names, it would have been impossible.

Could it really happen after all this time? As much as he didn't want to be disappointed, he couldn't stop the small sliver of hope that blossomed in his chest. He let out his breath and stepped to the window to look out over the city.

He inspected the buildings and streets for anything that seemed familiar, but came up empty. He was only seven or eight when he left, and he barely remembered anything from that time. This city was just as foreign to him as any other new place although, he had to admit, it was a lot more colorful.

Still, he felt no kinship or feeling that he was home. Of course, that might have something to do with what had happened to his father. If Rafael had been kidnapped and killed because of his ties to Cuba, then Ramos wanted nothing to do with this place.

He picked up his duffel bag and emptied the contents, hanging the dress jacket and a couple of shirts in the closet, and slipping the rest of his clothes into the dresser drawers. That task completed, he made sure his passport was safely tucked into his jacket pocket, along with the cash he'd brought.

A light knock sounded at the door, and Sloan came back inside carrying a folder. "Here it is." She handed him the folder, and he could hardly tear his gaze away from the sight of his father's name typed across the tab.

"I've got to go," Sloan said. "And I probably won't get back until late, but we can spend some time on it tomorrow."

"Sure." He glanced at her. "Thanks for this."

"Of course." She caught his gaze and stepped close. The light scent of her perfume brought unbidden memories of the short time they'd spent together all those months ago. Her eyes darkened with desire, and he dipped his head close enough to catch her lips with a teasing kiss.

She reached up and caressed his cheek before dropping her hand and pulling away. "You're making it hard to leave."

He smiled, hoping she couldn't see the effort it took for him to let her go. "That's the idea."

She shook her head, then gave him a saucy smile before leaving the room.

Chapter 10

After the door closed, Ramos let out a breath. She tempted him more than he let on, but that wasn't why he was here. Maybe they could spend a day or two together after this was over. Wait, that was stupid. He couldn't fall into a relationship with Sloan. It wasn't a good idea, even here in Cuba where she couldn't arrest him.

Too bad he couldn't turn off the desire that tugged at him every time he was with her. Grateful for the distraction, he took the folder to the small desk in the corner beside the billowing curtains, and pulled it open. The first thing that met his gaze was a photo of his father, probably taken the day they'd arrived in the states.

A shiver ran down his spine. Ramos had forgotten what his father looked like, but the similarities between them caught his breath. It also struck him that, in this photo, his dad was probably the same age as Ramos was right now.

He set the picture down and glanced through the paperwork, finding the form with his family's names and dates of birth. The next few pages consisted of copies of legal documents. The last page stated that his father had been a high-ranking officer in the Cuban military.

There was also a contact name listed of a Cuban-American in the states. The name was Geraldo Perez, and it stated that he had alerted the authorities to Rafael's kidnapping. He must have been the man who had helped his family after his father had disappeared. So why hadn't Geraldo told them the truth about his father's kidnapping? Maybe he'd told his mother and she'd kept it from him?

Below that, two addresses were listed. One was his family's former residence in Havana, and another was a contact for their next-of-kin. As Ramos read the names of his grandparents, a brief memory of sitting beside his grandmother came to his mind. He could almost hear her telling him to quit running off and be a good boy. He seemed to remember that she was always getting after him for something.

He closed his eyes and tried to remember more, but nothing else came. Maybe, once he found the house, it would all come back.

With growing excitement, he entered both addresses into his phone and used the app to find out how far away they were. He realized that the address of his home wasn't too far away from his hotel. Bursting with anticipation, he grabbed his black leather jacket and left the room.

It was close to six o'clock, and people jammed the streets, looking for places to eat and drink. The breezes coming off the ocean had turned cool, but pleasant. Most people wore the clothes and hats of tourists, so it was easy for him to differentiate between them and the native Cubans.

Slipping on his leather jacket, and wearing his jeans and a t-shirt, he fit in more with the Cubans. That brought a smile to his lips, and he decided to walk rather than take a taxi. The cobblestone streets in Old Havana were narrow anyway, and he wanted to get a feel for the place.

The sounds of a rumba-riff came from the side of the street, and he stopped to watch a man play his guitar. The strum-beat had a great rhythm, and he got caught up in it, moving his head to the tempo. The smells of tobacco were strong, and he could hardly keep up with the rapid Spanish that the natives spoke.

A few minutes later, he moved down the road and came upon a large open plaza filled with people and a small fountain bubbling in the center. The buildings surrounding the plaza were colorful and combined a baroque architecture with columns of blues, reds and yellows.

He continued through the center of this plaza and exited on the west side. The neighborhood he was looking for was called The Vedado, which meant "forbidden" in Spanish. As he got further away from Old Havana, he could see that this area was rich in historical relics of the past.

While many of these mansions had been turned into state offices and embassies, there were still several that were single-family homes. From the looks of them, they were on the more privileged side of the spectrum, even though everyone here was supposed to be treated equally.

He found the home he was looking for halfway down the street from a fenced-in "Casa Particular" which housed several families on different floors. The home he stood in front of was easily the most well-kept in the neighborhood, and looked like it had been recently updated.

What kind of family could afford to live in a place like this? Certainly it couldn't have belonged to his family? Nothing about the place brought memories to him of living there. Of course, if it had been re-done, that could explain it. Still, nothing about it seemed familiar. Wouldn't he have some memory if he'd lived there?

He stood in front of the house for several minutes, trying to decide if he should knock at the door. Then the door opened. A woman came out and stood on the broad porch.

She started toward the low gate between him and the house. "Are you lost?" she asked. Her kind face showed a few wrinkles, and her short, curly hair was streaked with silver. His breath caught to think that she could have easily been his own mother. She spoke in English, so Ramos knew he looked more American than he'd thought.

"I don't know. I think this is the house I'm looking for, but I'm not sure."

Her brows drew together. "What do you mean?"

Ramos smiled and shook his head apologetically. "I'm sorry. I had information that this home once belonged to a man by the name of Rafael Ramirez. Have you ever heard of him?"

Her smile faded, and her sharp gaze took in his features. Then she shook her head. "No. I don't know that name."

Ramos knew she was lying. But why? "He was an officer in the Cuban military, does that help?"

She took a deep breath and cocked her head. "Why are you looking for him?"

"Oh, I'm not looking for him. He died a long time ago. I was just wondering if any of his family was still here."

His explanation satisfied her, and her smile returned. "Now that you mention it, the name does sound familiar. He may have served with my husband at some point. Vincente served for many years before he transferred to an office job. Perhaps that is the connection."

Hope flared through Ramos's chest. "If he knew Rafael, I would like to speak with him. Is that possible?"

"Maybe. But first, you must tell me who you are, and why you want to know." She smiled and waited for his reply.

Ramos didn't think telling her his given name, along with his relationship to Rafael was a good idea, so he stuck with the truth as it was now. "My name is Alejandro Ramos. I was born here in Cuba, but my parents took me to America when I was just a kid. They're both dead now, but Rafael was my father's cousin." He smiled. "They told me he disappeared a long time ago, and I was curious about what happened to him."

From her frown, he wasn't sure using the word "disappeared" had been a good idea. Probably because that was the word they used to explain what happened to people who criticized the regime. "Is your husband at home?"

As she considered it, her lips thinned. Then she said, "Wait here. I will ask if he will see you, but I can't guarantee anything."

"Thank you." Ramos watched her enter the house. With a sigh, he turned and paced along the sidewalk in front of the house, his nerves on edge. Talking to this man shouldn't get him in trouble, and from the way the woman had spoken, he was pretty sure this man had known his father. Maybe they both had.

Ramos had almost given up when the door opened, and an older man stepped onto the porch. He glanced at Ramos and stopped short, then proceeded down the steps and toward the gate. He wore long, khaki pants and a button-up, short-sleeved shirt of nearly the identical color. If Ramos were to guess, he'd think it was a uniform of some kind.

His dark hair had more gray in it than his wife's, but he stood tall and walked toward Ramos like someone holding a great deal of authority. Stopping at the gate, he nodded and, although his lips tilted up, it was more of a grimace than a smile. It didn't surprise Ramos. This man's stony face gave the impression that he'd rather chew nails than crack a smile.

"Hello," he said. "When my wife told me you were asking about my old friend, Rafael Ramirez, I had to come and see you for myself. I haven't heard that name for a long time. Yanara said you were related?"

"Yes," Ramos answered. "I'm Alejandro Ramos. Rafael Ramirez was my father's cousin. So you knew him well?"

"Yes. We were in the military together." He swung the gate open and motioned to Ramos. "Come in and we'll talk. Let me introduce myself, I am Vincente Garcia." He held out his hand for Ramos to shake.

Ramos shook his hand, noting his firm grip and penetrating gaze. Vincente was nearly as tall as Ramos, but not quite as broad or strong. Still, his gaze left Ramos in no doubt that he commanded the situation and only spoke to Ramos because he wanted to.

"We will sit here on the porch, and I'll have Yanara bring us something to drink."

Ramos murmured his thanks and sat down in an old, comfortable chair. Vincente went inside and returned a moment later with Yanara following. She held a tray with two glasses, along with a bottle of rum, and set them on the small, round table between the chairs, then went back inside.

As she left, Vincente thanked her and poured the liquor into their glasses, then he raised his glass in a toast. "To Rafael."

Surprised, Ramos raised his glass as well. After clinking them together, he took a small swallow of the amber liquid, noting how smoothly it went down. Then he held the glass in his hand and waited for Vincente to start the conversation.

"So, tell me about yourself," Vincente began. "My wife said you were born in Cuba?"

"That's right, but I was young, and I don't remember much." Ramos didn't want to talk about himself, so he changed the subject. "So you were in the military with Rafael? What was he like?"

Vincente swirled the amber liquid around in his glass before taking another sip of his drink. Then he pulled a famous Cuban cigar from his pocket and lit it up. He offered one to Ramos, who politely declined. After taking a few puffs, he sent Ramos a quick glance and then continued the conversation.

"Rafael was a good soldier. We were in the same class and came up through the ranks together. He was a stubborn man. Some would say he was full of pride." Vincente shrugged. "But I think he was full of ideas. He was a thinker...but his ideas got him into trouble. I suppose that's why he left. After that, I never saw him again."

"And was this where he lived?" Ramos asked. Vincente glanced at Ramos like he was waiting for an accusation of some kind. Ramos kept silent, and Vincente's lips tightened before he nodded.

"Yes." Vincente glanced at the house and porch. "After Rafael left, they gave it to me, and I have lived here ever since."

Ramos sensed that there was much more to the story, but with Vincente's lips tightly closed, it was clear that the old man wasn't in the mood to share. Still, Ramos couldn't let him off that easily.

"Is there anything else you could tell me about him?"

Vincente sucked in a breath, then narrowed his gaze at Ramos, as if trying to decide how much to tell him. With a sigh, he glanced away and stared into the distance. From his rigid features, Ramos knew he was lost in the past. Then Vincente shook his head. "It is better to leave some things alone."

Ramos sighed, unhappy that Vincente wasn't willing to say more. But he figured there had to be a good reason. "Thanks for speaking with me, and for the drink."

Vincente nodded and glanced at Ramos with undisguised interest. "You look just like him," he said, surprising Ramos with his candor. Then he took another swallow of the amber liquid and stood, holding the cigar between his fingers. "How long will you be here in Cuba?"

"Another day, two at the most."

Vincente nodded. Then, keeping his gaze focused in the distance, he spoke. "I might have something that belonged to Rafael." He glanced at Ramos. "Why don't you come back tomorrow...around noon? I'll see if I can find it for you."

"Sure," Ramos agreed, and waited for Vincente to tell him more.

Instead, Vincente nodded and motioned Ramos toward the gate. "Good. I'll see you then."

Dismissed, Ramos walked to the street, feeling Vincente's gaze drilling a hole into his back. As he closed the gate, he glanced back at the house, but the porch stood empty. Taking a deep breath, he walked down the street until the house was out of sight. Then he paused and shook his head.

There was more to the story than Vincente had told him, and somewhere deep inside, he knew it wasn't good. Vincente's keen observation had recognized how much Ramos resembled Rafael. Would he put it together that Rafael was his father and not a cousin?

Now Vincente wanted Ramos to come back tomorrow. Did he really have something of his father's to give him? Or was there some other reason? From what he'd learned, he had a sinking feeling that Vincente knew more about his father's disappearance. Was he involved?

Ramos checked his watch. At six-forty, he decided it wasn't too late to take a chance of finding someone home at the other address. Using the directions from his phone, he began to walk deeper into The Vedado, and passed several mansions.

Some were in bad condition. They were falling apart and empty, which seemed strange. Others were in various stages of renovation. With some, the bottom level had been re-finished, but the top was in total disrepair. He realized that different families lived in each level, and it was easy to see which ones had more money.

Another mansion he passed had an eating establishment that covered the front lawn. Strings of lights crisscrossed over the tables, and people enjoyed all kinds of food. It reminded him that he had missed his dinner, but he was too close to stop now. He rounded the corner and paused. In front of him was the home he'd been looking for.

This mansion had three levels, which all looked about the same as far as repairs went. A large, double door marked the entrance, and several people sat outside on the steps. Ramos approached them and asked them in Spanish for the Ramirez family. A woman watching her three children told him they were on the third level and moved out of his way so he could go inside the building.

He found the graffiti-painted, central staircase and climbed to the third floor. A bright blue door awaited him at the top, and he took a breath before knocking. He heard sounds of running feet before the door flew open, and a small child stood in front of him. In Spanish, Ramos asked to speak to the child's mother, and the kid took off down the hall, leaving the door wide open.

A few minutes later, a woman who looked a few years younger than him came to the door. She glanced at Ramos, taking in his size, and alarm spread over her features.

Continuing in Spanish, Ramos told her he was looking for the relatives of Rafael Ramirez.

The woman's brows drew together at the mention of that name. "Are you from America?" she asked in English.

"Yes," he said, relieved that she spoke English. "Rafael Ramirez is my father." He'd never said that out loud to anyone, but it felt like the right thing to say.

The woman's breath caught, and her hand flew to her mouth. "Come in." She took hold of Ramos's arm and pulled him inside, then firmly shut the door. "Please come with me."

He followed her into a large living room painted in jewel tones with magenta on the walls and green potted plants in the corners. The marble floor shone from the golden hues of the sunset streaming through the large windows which overlooked the street, and something familiar unfurled in his memory. He'd been here before.

The woman glanced at him. "Stay here." She walked to the doorway that led into a kitchen and paused, not willing to let Ramos out of her sight. "Mama! Come quickly!"

He heard a muttered response from the other room, and a smattering of Spanish, before more footsteps sounded on the marble floor. Soon, a petite woman stood in the doorway holding a metal bowl she'd been wiping with a towel. Her dark gaze focused on Ramos, and her eyes widened with surprise.

"Rafael?" The bowl slipped from her fingers and clanged onto the floor, but she hardly noticed. Her breath hitched, and she took a couple of faltering steps toward him before she stopped and reason kicked in.

She shook her head, and Ramos worried that she might faint, so he closed the distance between them, taking her arm, and helping her sit on the couch. "I'm his son, Alejandro."

She shook her head in wonder, then reached up to touch his cheeks. "I never thought...I'm your Aunt Rosalyn, Rafael's sister." Her face broke into a smile, and tears filled her eyes. "I used to babysit you, but you probably don't remember. I can't believe it! How did you find us?"

"It's a long story," he said. "I didn't even know you existed until a few months ago."

"Why? Didn't your parents...what happened to all of you?"

Ramos took a breath, sure that his story would bring her pain, even if she needed to know. "Not long after we arrived in the states, my father left for work one day and never returned. He just...disappeared. I only found out a few months ago that he'd been brought back to Cuba against his will, so I came to find out what had happened to him."

Her eyes clouded over with sorrow, and she let out a breath. "So he's been missing all this time?"

"Yes."

She shook her head, and her eyes glistened with unshed tears. "We never heard from him, but I thought maybe the authorities had kept his letters from us. We always thought you were alive and well. But later...I wondered why nothing ever came, especially after our parents died. Are you sure he was brought back here?"

"It looks that way." As far as he was concerned, nothing had ever gone well for his family, not since his father had disappeared, and probably not before that either.

"Your mother, Isabel? And your brother, Javier? Are they..."

Ramos sucked in a breath. "Javier is fine, but my mother died a long time ago."

"Oh...that is...I'm so sorry. Poor Isabel. And Rafael...both of them...gone." She closed her eyes and swallowed, then pulled herself together and caught his gaze. "And you? Things are well with you?"

"I'm good." That came out more sharply than he'd intended, but Rosalyn just nodded her head. Then she smiled.

"I can't believe you are here. To find you after so long. It's a miracle." She glanced at her daughter and the two little boys who stood beside her. "Let me introduce you to your cousin and her children. This is Amara and her sons, Cedro and Rudi."

After they said hello to each other, Rosalyn turned to him. "Have you eaten? We just finished up our dinner, but we have plenty of food. Please...come into the kitchen. I'll fix you a plate and we can talk. I want to hear all about you and your life in the states."

That was the last thing Ramos wanted to tell her, but he was willing to go along with whatever she said. It was a lot to take in, and he could hardly believe he'd found his family. Entering the kitchen brought a brief feeling of familiarity, especially coupled with the smells of a home-cooked meal.

He took a seat at the kitchen table and observed the family's interactions. Rosalyn wore a purple-and-blue plaid apron over a blue shirt and slacks. She took charge of the food while Amara finished cleaning up the dishes.

The boys went back to playing with their toys. Cedro held a small plane in his hand and flew it around the room making engine-sounding noises. Rudi pushed his plane across the floor to take off into the air. They spoke to each other in Spanish, but Amara insisted they use English out of politeness to Ramos. She sent a happy smile his way and, for the first time since he'd come to Cuba, he felt like he belonged.

The boys took turns showing him their toys, and flew them all around the room in a competition that soon turned into a fight. Amara broke it up, then sent them to their room, threatening them with a bath if they didn't do as they were told.

Rosalyn brought over a huge plate of food and set it in front of Ramos. She handed him a knife and fork and told him to eat, then bustled off to get him something to drink. He dug into the food, enjoying the taste of the black beans and quinoa topped with spicy chicken, surrounded by fried, spicy bananas and mangos.

He had eaten half the food on his plate before he realized that he hadn't spoken a word. He glanced up to find Amara gone, and Rosalyn smiling with approval at his appetite. "This is really good. Thank you."

She nodded and continued to push a rag across the spotless counter. As he finished eating every crumb of food from his plate, Rosalyn poured them both a cup of coffee and set the cups down on the table with a carafe of milk and a bowl of sugar. She whisked his plate away to the sink and then sat down beside him. He leaned back in his chair. With his stomach full and satisfied, he smiled at her. "Best meal I've had in a long time."

"I'm glad you enjoyed it," Rosalyn said. She shook her head. "I still can't get over how much you look like Rafael. It's so good to have you here." Her eyes got misty, and she placed her hand on his arm, patting him with affection. "How's Javier?"

Ramos smiled, relieved that this was a subject he could talk about. Even though he hadn't spoken to Javier in ten years, he was grateful to know enough about him to sound like they had a relationship. It was easy to speak with pride of his brother's accomplishments.

Before she could ask him about himself, he changed the subject. "I need to ask you something. There was another address in the file they had on my father. It was listed as Rafael's home, so I went there first."

Rosalyn's smile faded, and her expression turned hard. "Did you talk to them?"

"Yes."

Her gaze sharpened. "Did you tell them who you were?"

"Not quite. I told them that my father was Rafael's cousin, but Vincente said I looked just like Rafael, so I don't know if it fooled him."

Rosalyn took a deep breath and let it out. "They were good friends once...Vincente and Rafael."

"What happened? He wouldn't tell me."

"What did he say?"

"Only that they were friends, but Rafael left, and he hadn't seen him since."

She shook her head and frowned, reluctant to speak of the past. "I suppose it's only right that you know the truth. Things went bad between them after the downfall of the Soviet Union. You have to understand that Cuba lost the Soviet subsidies we needed, and our economy collapsed. Because of that, all the government agencies were forced to cut back on many of the social services that we depended on.

"It got so bad that our food had to be rationed. We had constant electricity blackouts, and surpluses of everything disappeared. People suffered starvation and hardship. Do you know what Castro called it?"

Ramos shook his head, knowing it was a rhetorical question.

"A Special Period in Times of Peace." Rosalyn lowered her voice. "What a joke. A few changes were made, but it wasn't enough, and people were ready for something different...a new way of life. One of them was your father. As a member of the military, he saw first-hand how they were taking over the economy and creating a base of power for Raul Castro and his closest deputies, all while letting the people starve.

"So he began to speak out against the regime. A few friends joined him, then the word spread to others, and he gained a small following which began to grow into a movement. After a few months, some prominent people in the Cuban-American community got wind of his crusade and wanted to send money to get the word out. They even got the U.S. government involved."

She glanced at Ramos and shook her head. "It got him into trouble. Everyone distrusted the U.S. government, so it did him no good to take their money. It just escalated to the point where he was suspected of wanting the collapse of the Cuban government for his own gain."

She shook her head. "That was never his intention, but certain people saw it that way. They accused him of starting a rebellion so he could put himself in a place of power."

Ramos caught her gaze. "Let me guess...Vincente was one of them?"

She nodded, and her lips turned down with loathing. "I believe so. I think at first he supported Rafael. They had even made a plan together, but Vincente must have changed his mind." She whispered this so quietly that Ramos had to lean forward to hear her better.

"It wasn't long before someone brought Rafael to the attention of the government as the ringleader of the dissenters, and the regime planned to arrest him. Luckily, Rafael got wind of it and warned the others in his group. That night, he packed you all up and left for the states, using some of the money he'd obtained from a friend there.

He told me he was leaving and begged me not to tell anyone so our family wouldn't be punished.

"But, in the end, we lost our standing in the community. Your home belonged to your mother's family, and it was given away to someone more...deserving."

"Vincente," Ramos said.

Rosalyn nodded. "My father was spat upon for having a traitor for a son, even though he had served in the military for the revolution, but at least we were able to keep this place. Times were bad, but we always hoped that your family had escaped to a better life.

"We waited to hear from Rafael, but nothing ever came. We did get news from your mother's family that you had arrived and were safe, but they never spoke to us after that. We lost touch, and I'm not even sure what happened to them."

Ramos shook his head, troubled by this bleak picture. "After my father disappeared, a man helped us move from Miami to Orlando. In the file, it says that he was with Rafael and witnessed his kidnapping. Apparently, he barely escaped himself."

Rosalyn's eyes widened with horror. "You're sure Rafael was kidnapped?"

Ramos shrugged. "That's what the file says. Maybe he was killed that night. But if they brought him back to Cuba, then where is he? That's why I'm here. I need to find out what happened to him."

Rosalyn caught his gaze and shook her head. "No. You should stay out of it."

"But what if he's in prison somewhere?"

"He's not," she said sharply. "He can't be." Torment filled her eyes. "That long in prison? I can't bear to think of him suffering for so long."

"Then you think he's dead?" Ramos narrowed his eyes. "A life sentence for being a traitor isn't unusual."

"Traitors are hanged," she said. "There is no life sentence for that."

He glanced away, sorry he had upset her. Maybe he shouldn't have come. He made a move to stand, but Rosalyn grabbed his arm. "Please. Don't go. I'm fine. This has just been a shock."

He sat back in his chair and patted her hand. "I'm sorry to have upset you. I didn't mean to bring you pain."

"You have not brought me pain, querido. You are here, sitting in my kitchen, eating my food. It is wonderful. It's like having my brother back again. You are my family. You are my flesh and blood. Don't apologize for that."

A burst of warmth flooded Ramos's chest, and his eyes got misty. He blinked a few times and changed the subject. "Uh...tell me about Amara and the kids."

A smile brightened her face, and she sat back in her chair. She spoke about her daughter's family and stood to wash the dishes he had used. Ramos helped out by drying them, and he enjoyed hearing about the escapades of his cousin's children.

"We have a good life here," Rosalyn said. "Amara's husband is a chef, and he has a permit to run a restaurant that caters to all the tourists. He also has family in the states. We've thought about immigrating someday, but we'll see." She shrugged. "Cuba is our home."

Finished with clearing up, Rosalyn poured them both another cup of coffee, and they sat back down at the table. Amara soon joined them, happy to have the boys tucked into bed.

Ramos checked his watch, surprised it had gotten so late. "It's almost ten o'clock," he said. "I should go."

"No!" Rosalyn exclaimed. "Not yet. Stay a little longer. You haven't told us about yourself. We want to hear all about your life. What do you do?"

Ramos swore in his mind, but managed not to grimace too much. "I'm a security specialist for an investment firm. It's really not all that interesting, although they just sent me to Miami a few days ago. I got done with the job early, so that's why I'm here."

"And is there a woman in your life?" Amara asked. Rosalyn shushed her, but he could tell that she wanted to know just as much as Amara did.

"Not at the moment," he said, being as vague as possible.

Amara smiled knowingly and snorted a little. "That's code for none-of-your-business. But you can't fool me. You're a Ramirez...you probably have women throwing themselves at your feet on a constant basis. But don't worry, Mama." She glanced at her mother and patted her hand. "One of these days the right woman will come along, and that will be that."

They both smiled at him expectantly. His lips thinned and he raised a brow.

"Oooo...he's got the look down," Amara teased. "So full of himself."

"Amara, stop it," Rosalyn said, but her voice was soft.

"Well, ladies," Ramos began. "I can see that it's time to go." They began to protest, but he stood anyway. "Thank you for the food. It was delicious."

Rosalyn sighed and stood as well. "I hate to see you go, but I'm so happy you came." She followed him to the door. "Will you be back?"

"I don't know," he said. "But I'm happy I met you, and I'm glad you're doing well here." He turned to Amara. "You too."

Amara shook her head and pulled him into a big hug. "Take care, cousin. Come back any time." Giving him a sweet smile, she nodded at her mother and left the room.

Rosalyn studied Ramos's face, but didn't find what she was looking for. "You won't be back, will you?"

"No. I don't think so."

She nodded with resignation. "Stay away from Vincente. He's not someone you want to cross."

Ramos's gaze hardened. If Vincente was the reason his father was dead, then he'd make no such promises.

Rosalyn shivered and pulled Ramos into a tight hug. She held him close, just like he supposed a mother would, and it caught at his heart. After a moment, he hugged her back, taking a deep breath and catching the familiar scent of vanilla and jasmine. He hadn't smelled that since he'd left home and his mother behind.

Rosalyn patted his back before stepping away. "I think you've had a hard life, Alejandro. I wish I could have been there for you. But remember this...you are loved, and you are always welcome here."

The ice around his heart began to melt, but he strengthened his resolve, knowing he could never let anyone he cared about into his world. "Thanks Rosalyn." He sent her a nod and opened the door.

She moved to stand in the doorway and watched him walk away. "A word of advice," she called. He turned to glance back at her. She let out a breath and glanced away, unsure of her words. Coming to a decision, she caught his gaze. "Don't sell your soul for a lost cause. Your father wouldn't want that for you, and neither do I."

As a trained killer, it was already too late for that, but he was grateful that she didn't know the truth. It was better to let her think the best of him, so she could remember him in a good light. He sent her an appreciative nod and hurried down the stairs.

He didn't look back.

Chapter 11

Out on the street, Ramos meandered back the way he'd come. It was full dark, but there were enough lights to see where he was headed. On impulse, he headed toward Vincente's home again. As he neared the house, he stopped across the street and watched from the shadow of a big palm tree.

It was hard to believe he had ever lived there, but it had to be true. If it had once belonged to his mother's family, he had no idea how to look for them now. The home was large enough to house two or three families, but Vincente had it all to himself.

A car turned the corner and drove toward him. Ramos ducked behind the tree so he wouldn't get caught in the headlights. It pulled over to stop right in front of Vincente's house. A man in a police officer's uniform climbed out. Holding something in his hand, he opened the gate and strode to the front door.

A few minutes after knocking, Vincente opened the door. He stepped onto the broad porch and they spoke for a minute. From Ramos's spot, he couldn't hear what they said, but the police officer held up a folder and handed it to Vincente.

Vincente opened the folder, then nodded and clapped the officer on the back. After a few more words, the officer left, and Vincente went back inside and closed the door. Ramos hid again from the car's lights and, once it had gone, he glanced back at the house.

A light switched on in a corner room on the second story. The drapes weren't closed all the way, and Ramos caught a glimpse of Vincente inside, reading the information that had just been delivered. Then he moved out of sight and the light switched off.

Ramos watched for a few more minutes but, with nothing more to see, he decided to head back to the hotel. Did this late-night rendezvous have something to do with his visit? Vincente had told Ramos that he had something of his father's to show him. After talking to Rosalyn, he wasn't sure if it was true, or just a ruse to lure him back.

He walked purposefully toward old town Havana. Coming to an intersection bustling with people, he hailed a taxi and rode the rest of the way back to the hotel. Once inside, he climbed the stairs rather than taking the elevator. Outside his door, he pulled out his key card. As he pushed it inside the slot, the door gave way, signaling that it hadn't shut properly.

Alarm prickled at the back of his neck. Had someone broken into his room? Anger poured over him, and he pushed the door open, then cautiously stepped inside. Nothing seemed out of place, and he was grateful he'd taken the time to hide the file on his father.

After tightly shutting and locking his door, he checked the bathroom and closets to make sure he was alone. Next, he checked behind the headboard where he'd left the file.

Finding it safe, his shoulders relaxed, and he let out a breath.

Then he noticed that his duffel bag had been moved, and the clothes in the drawers weren't as tidy as he'd left them. But nothing was missing. Good thing he'd kept his passport with him, along with all the cash he'd brought.

So who had broken into his room? Did it have something to do with the police officer at Vincente's house? The officer had given Vincente some papers, but that didn't mean it had anything to do with Ramos.

He wished he knew what job Vincente held. His wife had said he had been in the military but now worked at a desk job. Did Vincente have the resources to look into Ramos's visit? Ramos had given Vincente his name, so it was possible.

With nothing left to be done, he made sure the door was secure in case he had any more visitors, and got ready for bed. He read through the file more thoroughly, hoping to find something he'd missed. When nothing came of that, he turned out the light, more determined than ever to meet with Vincente the next day. He needed to know more about him and his connection to his father. If Vincente knew what had happened to Rafael, Ramos was determined to find out.

But what would he do about it? That was the question that kept him awake most of the night. What if it was Vincente who'd turned his father in? Was Ramos ready to kill him for it? If his father was dead, did it matter?

But if his father was alive...no, it didn't seem possible. How could he be alive after so long? But if he was, Ramos had to do everything in his power to find him, even if it meant beating it out of Vincente. Then he'd decide what to do.

Early the next morning his phone rang. He pulled himself out of a half-slumber and answered on the fourth ring. "Hello?"

"Hey Ramos," Sloan said. "I just thought I'd check in with you. You want to get breakfast?"

"Sure."

"Meet me in the lobby in twenty minutes."

"Okay," Ramos agreed and disconnected. He jumped in the shower and got ready for the day. In the lobby, he only waited a few minutes before Sloan appeared. Looking casual with her dark, wavy hair flowing around her face, and wearing straight-leg jeans and a tightly-fitted shirt, she caught the attention of every man in the lobby.

She came by herself, and it relieved him that he didn't have to face her partner. Still, he wouldn't mind knowing a bit more about him. "Where's your partner?"

"Noah's busy," she said, lifting her shoulder in a dismissive shrug. "There's a great place to grab some breakfast about a block away. We can talk more there."

"Lead the way."

He walked beside her to a café down the street, keeping an eye out for anyone following them. Of course, that was a little difficult, since more than one man gave Sloan a second glance. It was beginning to irritate him. As an agent, wasn't she supposed to try and blend in?

With only a few patrons inside the café, Ramos asked for a table in a corner for some privacy. After sitting down, they were given menus to look over. Since Ramos wasn't real hungry after the big dinner he'd eaten the night before, he ordered the traditional Cuban breakfast of Café con Leche with tostada bread and some fruit.

Sloan smiled at him and did the same. "This is my favorite breakfast. It's one of the things I love about being here."

"I vaguely remember having it while I was growing up."

The server brought a mug of warm milk and a small metal carafe of strong, Cuban coffee. The server also set a bowl of fruit in front of each of them, along with the flat, buttered bread, and then left them to eat in privacy.

Pouring the coffee into the milk, Ramos created his own latte and added a spoonful of sugar. Without thinking, he took a piece of the bread and dipped it into his coffee, only realizing afterward that he hadn't eaten his bread dipped in coffee like that since he'd lived at home with his mother.

It sent a powerful wave of nostalgia through him that nearly took his breath away. Needing to suppress those unwanted feelings, he glanced at Sloan, grateful for the distraction of a beautiful woman. He took in her lovely face, and found that her easy smile relieved his melancholy.

"So how did things go last night?" he asked Sloan. She bit her lip, a sure sign that she needed something from Ramos, and he tensed.

"Good. My contact gave us some great information. But...uh...I might need your help."

He huffed out a breath and raised his right brow. "How's that?"

Sloan leaned forward and spoke quietly. "From the little I gathered, he has a pretty good idea about what's going on. After we negotiated his price, we set up a dead drop. That's where Noah is right now. If our contact comes through with good intel, I might need your help with the follow-up."

"What about Noah? Why isn't he the one helping you?"

"Oh, he is, but he's obviously not Cuban. He might stand out. I could do this without you, but I think you and I would have a better chance of succeeding than I would by myself. You don't have to help me, but I was hoping you'd at least think about it."

He sipped his coffee and caught her gaze. He didn't like the idea of her going it alone, but he didn't want to get involved. "If I agreed, you'd have to let me in on what's going on. That means everything. No secrets this time."

She flinched with guilt. "You'll know everything that I know. I promise."

Ramos nodded, but he had his doubts that Noah was on board. Still, Sloan had a way of getting what she wanted. "What would I have to do?"

She let out a relieved breath and smiled. "Not much. From what we know so far, it's more of a reconnaissance mission." She glanced around the café. "We'll go over everything back at the hotel."

He nodded, understanding that she could only say so much in public. He hoped she realized that he hadn't said he'd do it. And he wasn't about to get pushed into something, no matter how easy she said it was.

"So, how about you?" she asked, changing the subject. "What did you do last night?"

"I went to the addresses in the file."

Her eyes widened with interest. "Did you find anything?"

"Yes. I found out I have an aunt. She's my father's sister, and I met my cousin and her family."

"Wow, that's great. What was it like?"

"It was good," he said. "She had no idea my father had disappeared, but she'd always wondered why she hadn't heard from us for so long. It was nice, but kind of hard, too." Not wanting to go into any more details, he continued. "I found an older couple living at the other address. I spoke with the man, and he told me that he knew Rafael."

"Did you tell him who you were?"

"Not exactly," Ramos said. "I decided to tell him that Rafael was my father's cousin. He told me that he and Rafael were old friends who went their separate ways before my father came to the states. He didn't give away anything, but I think he knows more than he would say."

"What's his name?" Sloan asked.

"Vincente Garcia."

Sloan's eyes widened, and she sucked in a breath, nearly choking on her food. "You actually spoke with him?"

"Yes. Why?"

She gaped at Ramos with undisguised alarm. "I've heard of him. He's the head of the Cuban police, only...it's the part of the police that's more like the KGB. He has a lot of power. We think he's probably been involved with the arrests of any Cubans who have spoken out against the regime."

Dread washed over Ramos. That meant he was more involved with Rafael than he let on. "Now it makes sense. Last night someone looked through my things while I was gone, but nothing was taken."

Sloan gasped. "Did they see the file?"

"No. I hid it before I left, and it hadn't been touched."

"That's a relief." Sloan chewed on her bottom lip. "It must have been Vincente checking up on you."

Ramos nodded. "My aunt thinks he might have had something to do with my father's disappearance. She told me to stay away from him."

"That's a good idea."

Ramos shrugged. "Maybe...but he invited me to come back today at noon."

"What? Why?"

"He said he might have something that belonged to Rafael that he wanted to give me."

Sloan's brows drew together, and she shook her head. "I don't like it. I mean...why would he do that? Is there a chance he knows who you are?"

"Maybe." Ramos shrugged. "But what can he do? Besides, I need to find out what he knows about my father. So I'm going." He leveled a hard stare her way so she'd know he couldn't be talked out of it. "Do you think it might ruin your plans?"

"Uh..." she shook her head. "I don't think so, but I'll know more after I talk to Noah."

Ramos nodded, then finished off his tostada and checked his watch. He had nearly two hours before his meeting with Vincente, and he needed a break from all the drama. "Do you want to help me get some Cuban cigars for Manetto?"

Sloan's mouth widened in surprise, then she chuckled. "Sure. They only sell the good ones in the Casa del Habana store, but it's not far."

After they settled the bill, Sloan took Ramos by the arm. As they strolled down the street, Sloan's light touch wasn't overbearing or possessive, allowing Ramos to relax and enjoy the attention. She took him to the store where he purchased a box of cigars for Manetto, along with a special lighter.

From there they took their time, acting just like regular tourists. He enjoyed the reprieve and found it easy to slip into the role of a couple. They stopped to listen to a street performer playing his guitar. When he started playing the chorus they both chimed in, surprising each other that they both knew the words.

Sloan spoke of her parents and her life in Miami and Little Havana, and how she grew up on those songs and many of the foods and traditions of Cuba. Hearing that, Ramos wondered if he would have met her if he'd stayed there instead of moving to Orlando. His life might have been so different if his father had been in the picture.

Ramos relaxed his guard, finding that their easy banter and talk of the past brought back the companionship they'd shared when they'd first met. At a tourist shop, Sloan laughed to find a nunchuck pen set which reminded her of the time she'd used something very similar on Ramos, and laid him out flat. She couldn't resist teasing him about it, and ended up buying it for him.

Leaving the shop, she wrapped her arm around his waist and he pulled her against his side. Smiling, they turned down the street and ducked into the next shop. While Sloan glanced through a display of scarves, Ramos found a monkey made out of coconut shells sitting on a shelf with a tiny cigarette hanging out of its mouth. It was so typical of Cuba that it brought a smile to his lips. He thought of getting it for Shelby, then shook his head. Why was he thinking of Shelby when he had a beautiful woman right in front of him?

He glanced at Sloan, admiring her quick smile and flashing eyes. Her hair cascaded in waves over her shoulders, and she presented an alluring picture that enchanted him. She caught him staring at her and sent him a slow smile. It brought him up short, and he shook his head. What was he doing?

Sloan came to his side and took his arm. "What's that?" she asked, picking up the monkey. She grinned up at him. "He's kind of cute. Are you going to get him for me?"

"What? No way. Total waste of money."

She chuckled, and set it back down. "You're probably right." Taking in his sullen expression, she tugged at his arm. "Hey, let's walk down to the beach. I haven't been there yet and I want to see it."

Ramos let her tug him out of the shop, and pushed his misgivings away. They strolled down the street toward the beach and he enjoyed the fresh breezes coming off the ocean.

"It's peaceful here," Sloan said, slipping her arm around his waist. Ramos let out a sigh, and wrapped his arm around her shoulders. Sure, he didn't want to admit how much he liked her company, but it would never be more than that, so why not enjoy it while he could?

They came to the end of the path with the stone wall overlooking the ocean. Ramos let her go and leaned against the wall, taking in the blue sky and ocean. Sloan did the same, closing her eyes to enjoy the breeze.

She turned toward him. "Do you ever wonder what would have happened between us if things had been different?"

He glanced at her with narrowed eyes. "You mean if I wasn't a hitman for a mob-boss?"

She shrugged and shook her head. "I mean if you'd stayed here, or if we'd met in Miami. I don't know, it seems like we might have crossed paths somehow."

"It doesn't do any good to think like that."

"I know. But sometimes I wonder. Do you think that maybe there's..." Sloan's phone began to ring, stopping her in mid-sentence.

Ramos let out a relieved breath, grateful for the interruption. Sloan's lips twisted with annoyance, but she dutifully dug her phone out of her bag and answered it. From her tone, Ramos knew she was talking to Noah.

Ending the conversation, she slipped the phone back into her bag and glanced at Ramos. "That was Noah. He's back at the hotel with the information we've been waiting for. I'll probably need to spend the rest of the day with him figuring things out."

Ramos nodded and checked his watch. He didn't have time to go back to the hotel before his meeting with Vincente. "You go ahead. I'll let you know when I'm done with my meeting."

"Okay. Should I take your bag back to the hotel for you?"

"Oh, yeah that would be great." He handed her the box of cigars. After taking it, Sloan held onto his hands and glanced up at him.

"Good luck," she said, concern and worry filling her eyes.

"Thanks." He knew she wanted to kiss him, and had been flirting with him all morning. But it was the worry in her gaze that caught at his heart. Letting out a breath, he threw caution to the wind and captured her lips in a searing kiss filled with forbidden desire.

Then he pulled away and hardened his heart. Sure it was nice having someone concerned about him, but he had to face reality, and so did she. "I don't want to hurt you Sloan. You know this isn't going anywhere. It can't."

She let out a breath and swallowed. Then dark fire sparked in her eyes. "I know that. And it's not. Call me when you're done."

He would have believed her denial if that kiss hadn't affected her so deeply. It was easy to see the warm flush in her cheeks, and the dazed look in her eyes. With a lift of his brow, he sent her a quick nod.

Her eyes flashed and she turned on her heel, retracing her steps back to the hotel. He watched her for a long minute before following the stone wall to a bridge he could cross. Letting out a breath, he shook his head. Being with Sloan was just asking for trouble, and he should know better than to let his guard down around her.

Pushing thoughts of Sloan from his mind, he retraced his steps from the day before, crossing through the square and into The Vedado. In the full light of day, he noticed the tall palm trees and flowering bushes surrounding the estates that he'd missed the night before. Away from the crowds and smell of tobacco, the air carried an earthy scent.

Though not as crowded here, there were still plenty of people out. It reminded him that Vincente might have him followed, so he made sure to keep track of the people around him. As he arrived at the house this time, he opened the gate and strode straight up the steps to the front door.

After a quick knock, it wasn't long before the door opened and Vincente's wife, Yanara, greeted him with a smile. "Please come in," she said, opening the door wide. He preceded her into the house, noting the high ceilinged room with arching doorways and wainscoting around the ceiling and floor.

A flash of recognition brought him up short, then just as quickly left. He knew he'd been there before, but he couldn't seem to remember any details.

"Please sit down," she said, motioning to the couch in the large living room.

Instead of leaving to get Vincente, she sat down in a winged-back armchair and smiled at him. "I'm sorry to tell you that Vincente isn't here, but he found something that he wanted me to give you."

As Yanara stood to retrieve the item, Ramos's chest constricted with disappointment. He let out a resigned breath and glanced at the woman. If Vincente knew his father, she might have known him too. Maybe she would be more forthcoming than Vincente if Ramos poured on the charm.

She returned with a small, square box and handed it to Ramos. "It's not much, but there are a few things inside that belonged to Rafael." She smiled encouragingly. "Go ahead and open it."

Ramos let out a breath and gently pulled off the lid. Several photographs were stacked inside, along with two or three envelopes holding letters. As he pulled out the photos, he caught sight of a medal hanging from a worn, striped ribbon.

He turned his attention back to the photos, drinking in the pictures of his father standing proudly in a military uniform with a much younger Vincente by his side. The next few photos had both of his parents standing together, with his mother wearing a white wedding dress. They smiled with happiness, and a stab of pain pierced Ramos's heart.

"That was on the day of their wedding," Yanara said. "They were so happy."

"You knew both of them?"

"Oh, sí, very well."

Ramos glanced through several more pictures of the wedding party, wondering who all of the people were, and if they were his relatives. He thought one of the younger women looked like his Aunt Rosalyn. Then he came to another photo of his parents with his mother holding a baby.

"Their oldest son," Yanara said. She glanced at Ramos, studying him with pointed interest. "They were overjoyed to have a baby boy."

Ramos swallowed and glanced at the next photo. It was of him as a young child, probably around two years old. His father knelt down next to him with a smile of joy on his face, and Ramos was reaching to touch his face with his small fingers. The love in his father's gaze reached out to him, catching his breath and filling his heart.

The last photo showed him a little older, standing in front of his parents and holding his father's hand. His mother held a baby in her arms. His brother. Ramos's throat tightened, and he quickly shoved the photos into a stack before setting them back in the box.

Yanara glanced at him with curiosity.

Ramos took a moment to get under control, then he met Yanara's gaze and tried to give her a relaxed smile. "These are great." He glanced down into the contents of the box and pulled out the medal, hoping to get Yanara to talk. "What was this for?"

"Let me see." She took the medal from him and examined it. "This is very old. It probably belonged to Rafael's father. He took part in the Cuban Revolution, you know. He was a very important man in the military."

"What about Rafael? Do you know why he left Cuba?"

Yanara let out a breath and shook her head. "He loved Cuba. I know that much. But I think he had other ideas that were not good. It was hard on Vincente when your father..." She glanced at Ramos with wide eyes. Then she smiled, and let out a chuckle. "I'm sorry, but you look just like him. It was not hard to guess. Please...take these. They belong to you."

Ramos didn't deny it, and relief poured over him that she knew the truth. "Do you know what happened to him?"

She shook her head, and her eyes darkened with wariness. "No." She glanced away before catching his gaze. "You should go back to your home in the states. Live your life. There is nothing here for you."

Surprised at her vehement denial, he could only believe that she knew his father was dead. He glanced back at the photos, then nodded his head, and slipped the lid back on the box. "Thanks for this."

She nodded and smiled, but it was filled with sadness. He rose to leave, tucking the box under his arm and she followed him to the door. As he stepped onto the porch, he turned back to her with a nod of thanks. She took a breath, and glanced toward the street. "I meant what I said. Go home."

Before he could respond, she closed the door.

Chapter 12

Ramos knew she was warning him, but from what? Why would anyone in Cuba care about him? He made it back to the hotel and stepped into his room. After a quick glance around, he knew his things were where he'd left them.

He set the box on his bed and put a call through to Sloan. "I'm back."

"Great," she said. "How'd it go?"

"Fine. Not what I expected, but I think it helped."

"Good. Uh, I'm right in the middle of working out a strategy. Can we meet in an hour or two? I'll know more by then, and I'll be able to share everything with you."

Ramos checked his watch. It was just after one p.m. "Sure. Call me when you're free." She agreed, and they disconnected.

Ramos let out a breath, then opened the box and studied the photos more carefully. He closed his eyes and tried to place the faces to a memory, but they were like strangers to him. Those quick flashes of his father were no more than a shadow in his mind. Even his mother wore such a happy expression that he hardly recognized her.

Remembering nothing more, he pulled out his bag and placed everything from the box inside a zippered compartment. Then he took out his phone and pulled up the Internet. In the search engine, he typed the words, "Prisons in Cuba." Glancing through the responses, he found one called the "Villa Marista," which was said to house political dissidents.

Was this where his father had been taken? He pulled up the address and found that it wasn't far, just on the outskirts of Havana. With time on his hands, he decided to take a ride past the place, just to see what it looked like.

He locked up his room and headed down to the lobby of the hotel. The concierge, a middle-aged woman, was eager to help him. He asked if there was a car or motorcycle available to rent. "Si, we have car rentals nearby." She told him where to go, even saying that he'd probably find a scooter there that would fit his taste.

He thanked her before cringing at the idea of riding a scooter. With several taxis on the lookout for paying customers, it was easier to find a ride with one of them than rent a car.

After getting in, he told the driver that he only had an hour or so, and wanted to see the sights. He hoped that, during the ride, he could ask about the Villa Marista without seeming too obvious.

Ramos actually enjoyed the ride through Havana, and his driver was more than happy to give a guided tour, especially since he was able to do so in Spanish. They drove past the National Capitol Building, and then the baroque Catedral de San Cristóbal and Plaza Vieja, whose buildings reflected the city's vibrant architectural mix.

They also drove by La Cabaña, an 18th-century fortress complex that stood watch over the eastern side of the harbor entrance. With the hour almost gone, Ramos finally asked if they could drive by the Villa Marista.

The driver's gaze jerked to the rear-view mirror, glancing at Ramos with sudden understanding. He gave Ramos a quick nod and agreed to drive past the compound. The driver didn't speak again until they reached the Villa, then he pointed it out while slowing the car to a crawl.

The gray block building was surrounded by a tall fence with razor wire along the top. A guard station stood beside the closed gate. All the windows along the side of the building were barred, and a state of neglect and despair hung heavy over the scene.

As they drove away, the driver told Ramos that the Villa had once been a Catholic seminary, but was now used as an interrogation center. He glanced once more at Ramos and told him that it was said that the interrogation techniques learned from the KGB eventually made everyone "sing" who ended up there.

Ramos's stomach clenched with the sick feeling that, if his father had ended up there, he was probably long dead by now. At least he fervently hoped that was the case. He couldn't imagine living in that hell for all these years.

Then there was Vincente. If he was the head of the police with their KGB tactics, could he have been the one who'd masterminded his father's kidnapping after all? Had he killed his father?

The driver interrupted Ramos's thoughts, asking him where he'd like to go next. Ramos had seen enough of Cuba to last him for a long time. He thanked the driver for the tour and asked to be taken back to his hotel.

Getting out of the taxi, Ramos thanked the driver again and gave him a generous tip, then headed back to his room. With a heavy heart, Ramos was more than ready to return to his normal life. He would accomplish nothing by killing

Vincente and, like his aunt had said, his father wouldn't have wanted that. He'd want Ramos as far from this place as he could get.

Ramos got back to his room and packed up his things, ready to put this all behind him. As he finished up, his phone rang.

"Hey Ramos," Sloan said. "Can you come to my room?"

He wanted to tell her that he was leaving, but decided it would be better to tell her in person. "Sure. I'll be there in a minute."

He knocked on the door, expecting to see Sloan. Instead, the door was opened by a man wearing shorts and a t-shirt. He had a short beard and close-cropped hair, but he wasn't as tall or as muscular as Ramos, and his eyes narrowed with distaste.

Ramos wasn't sure how long they would have stared at each other, but Sloan quickly pushed Noah out of the way and beckoned Ramos inside. He entered the room with misgiving. This wasn't his job. What was he doing here?

"Thanks for coming," Sloan said, smiling with encouragement. She glanced at Noah, and her expression hardened. "Noah, get over it."

Noah twisted his lips and shook his head, but didn't move away. "So this is your boyfriend. You think he's going to help us?"

"Noah! Stop it. We need him."

With a resigned sigh, Noah turned away and threw himself into a chair, rubbing his head with his hands. "You're right. Sorry Sloan. I just have a hard time working with a criminal."

Ramos held back a chuckle, but he couldn't suppress his smile. This guy was a straight arrow, and he felt a little sorry for Sloan. "What's going on?"

"Let me bring you up to date with what we have," she began. "A few months ago, our source found an exchange between a Cuban government official and a known Russian operative. They spoke about the performance of the gift the official had been given, and how it had exceeded his expectations. Our source believes it has something to do with the attacks on our embassy. We set up a dead drop where he left us some vital intel."

Sloan folded her arms and began to pace back and forth. "With this information, we can get eyes on the device."

Ramos caught her gaze. "Device? What kind of device?"

"We don't know, exactly. That's why we need to get in there to see it. But, from everything we know, we think it is some kind of a sonic device. All of our embassy workers who have suffered problems heard multiple, high-pitched, shrieking noises."

"Were they directed at the embassy?"

"No. Our diplomats were targeted in their own homes. Right after the attacks, they reported severe symptoms including deafness, vision problems and difficulty concentrating. But no one can figure out what would cause that unless it's some kind of a sonic device. Even our scientists are stumped. If we can get a look at it, we'd have a better idea of what we're dealing with."

Sloan opened a folded blueprint and tapped her finger on the part circled in red. "This is an old mansion that's not far from our diplomat's home. It's also close to Old Havana and most of the embassies. This circled room is on the lower floor in the back.

"The mansion is used as a government office building. The upper floors are for the housing department. Since a lot of people go in and out of there, getting inside isn't a problem. But we need to go to the lower level, and that's a problem because there's more security there."

"That's why we need you," Noah said, glancing at Ramos. "Our source left a couple of ID badges to get inside the room on the lower level. You'd pass as Cuban, where I wouldn't." He held up the ID badges, which dangled from black lanyards. "Luckily, I have the equipment to doctor these up with photos of you, so it shouldn't be a problem."

"Shouldn't? Do you even know what kind of security we'd have to pass through?" Ramos asked.

"Some," Sloan said. "My source said the badges would get us into the room without a problem, but I don't know what kind of security is on the lower floor."

"I've spent a lot of time observing the building," Noah added. "From what I could see, the employees work a regular eight-to-five day. I think using the badges is a better idea than trying to break in after dark."

"I think we need to move on this now," Sloan said. "How soon can you get the badges ready?"

"Not long," Noah answered.

"Why so soon?" Ramos asked.

Sloan shrugged. "I don't know. It's just a feeling I have that we need to get this done, before anything jeopardizes the mission, or they move the device. If something happened to our source, we'd miss our chance. We've known about the building for a couple of days, so we've been observing it. I even changed my appearance and went inside to the housing department, so I know what to expect. We just didn't have a way into the lower level until now." She glanced at Ramos. "What do you think? Will you help me?"

Ramos let out a breath. This whole thing seemed rushed, and he didn't like feeling pressured. But, as much as he didn't want to get involved, he also didn't like the idea of Sloan going in there without him.

Seeing his hesitation, she continued. "It would just be a matter of slipping inside. Once we're in the room, we can grab the device and then get out."

Ramos shook his head. She thought that would be easy? "What if it's too big to move?"

"I think it has to be portable since it was used at the diplomats' homes. But if it's too big, then I guess we'll have to get creative and break it or something. At the very least, we can take photos of it."

The hope in Sloan's gaze made it hard for Ramos to let her down. "I guess I can help you, as long as there's a way out that doesn't include getting caught."

"Of course," Sloan said, her eyes lighting up with excitement. "That's where Noah comes in. He'll cause a diversion if we need it."

"I'll be monitoring you the whole time," Noah said. "I think if you enter the building just before the work day ends, you could leave at the same time as everyone else. Then, if something happened, you'd have a better chance of getting lost in the crowd."

"That should work," Sloan said, checking her watch. "We have two hours before five o'clock. Why don't we get started on those ID badges?"

As they followed Noah to his room, Ramos could hardly believe that he'd agreed to help Sloan. Again. She'd barely given him a moment to think it through. And he'd agreed. What was wrong with him? In Noah's room, Ramos glanced her way, watching as Noah set up his equipment and took her picture.

It wasn't just her beauty he admired, although he could get lost in the depths of her smoky eyes. She believed in something bigger than herself, and she was good at what she did. If they were on the same side, they'd be great partners. He liked that she knew how to fight and handle a gun. Beyond that, there was the physical attraction that pulled him to her and made him ready to throw caution to the wind just to hold her in his arms.

He shook his head, finally admitting that he cared for her. That was a huge problem.

Noah took Ramos's picture and kept telling him not to scowl so much, but it was a lost cause. No way could Ramos even try to look pleasant with that on his mind.

"While I get these ready, you guys will need to change into some business clothes," Noah said. He glanced at Ramos. "Do you have some slacks and a nice shirt? I might have something if you don't."

"I've got it covered," Ramos said, not about to borrow anything from him.

"Okay. Good."

Sloan left the room with Ramos following close behind. She stopped in front of her door and turned to him. "Come in for a minute. We need to talk."

Ramos didn't like the sound of that. He also didn't like the invitation into her room. What did she want? Right now, she had gotten more out of him than he wanted to give. Maybe it wasn't too late to back out?

"It won't take long." Her determined gaze held his, and Ramos knew she wouldn't back down. With resignation, he nodded and followed her inside the room.

As soon as the door closed, she began. "Look, I appreciate your help with this, but if you don't want to go through with it, I understand."

Ramos twisted his lips and let out a frustrated breath. "If I thought you'd be okay without me, I wouldn't be helping you." It was the truth. This was her job, and getting caught up in it was the last thing he wanted to do.

Sloan's breath caught, and he was pretty sure he'd just insulted her. "Fine. I get it. You can just stay here."

"No," Ramos said, grabbing her arms. "I'm coming with you, but this is the last time."

Sloan pulled out of his grasp. "Never mind. I can do it without you."

"No you can't," Ramos said. "You need me for this, and I'm coming. I just need you to understand the position this puts me in."

Sloan lowered her eyes and let out a breath. "You're right. I am asking a lot. Once we're done, I'll never ask anything of you again."

Ramos nodded. "Good. I can live with that." He turned to leave, but Sloan caught his arm.

"Wait. Don't go yet." He turned to face her and she dropped his arm, then took a breath and glanced up at him. "You have to tell me how things went with Vincente. Did you find out what happened to your father?"

It was plain to see that she wanted to know because she cared about him. A part of him wanted to push her away, but he couldn't do it. He wanted her to know. He wanted to share this with her, because it was important to him. "Vincente wasn't there, but I talked to his wife. I'm pretty sure my father's dead. She told me to go home. I don't think she would have said that if he was still alive."

Sloan nodded. "Do you think she knows what happened to him?"

"Yeah, I do." He let out a big sigh and shook his head. "She's hiding something. It might be that Vincente was involved in my father's death and she's protecting him. I don't know. I'm not even sure it matters anymore." There was a part of him that would always wonder what had happened to his father, but looking into a past filled with pain was taking a toll on him.

Sloan stepped close and put her arms around him, offering him comfort that took him by surprise. After a couple of seconds, he gave in to the temptation to hold her close, and inhaled the scent of her perfume that always made him think of moonlight and shadows. With reluctance, he let out a breath. "We can't do this."

She sighed, but kept her arms around his waist. "Do what?"

"You and me." Whether they were in Cuba or not, being in a relationship with her was just asking for trouble. Look at the situation he was in now. He couldn't live like this. He stepped away, but she wouldn't let him go.

"Ramos, wait. This is the last time I'll involve you in my work. I'll never ask for your help again. I promise. And it's okay if we're never together. I don't want that, but I'd like to spend some time with you. I don't expect anything permanent, but one night in Cuba wouldn't be so bad would it?"

He closed his eyes and huffed out a breath. "And you can just forget me?"

Her lips twisted and she shrugged. "Does it matter?"

"Of course it matters. What I do, what you do. It all matters." He pulled her arms from around him and held them in a firm grip, wishing he could shake some sense into her, and gazed fiercely into her eyes. "I don't want to care about you."

She opened her mouth to speak, but it was too much. He gave in to his desire and lowered his lips to hers in a searing kiss. She responded just as desperately, and they clung to one another, all that pent-up tension rocketing through them. The kiss deepened, and Ramos wasn't sure he could stop, or even if he wanted to.

Several loud knocks on the door brought their scorching kiss to an end, and they broke apart. Heart pounding and breathless, he let her go. Sloan took several deep breaths, then managed to glance through the peep hole.

"It's Noah," she whispered.

Ramos nodded and leaned against the door frame, then folded his arms over his chest and let out his breath. Sloan opened the door a crack to speak to Noah, but he barged inside. He nearly jumped a foot to find Ramos standing there.

Before Noah could say a thing, Ramos straightened. "Don't worry. I'm leaving." With a glance at Sloan, he stepped out the door.

"Wait," she called. He turned back, and she grabbed the package holding the cigars and nunchucks from her dresser. "Don't forget this."

She was trying to make it look like the package was the reason he'd stopped by. Ramos glanced at Noah, and knew it hadn't fooled him. With a nod, Ramos took the package and headed down the hall to the stairs. He hurried down them to the floor below, using the physical exertion to help release his pent-up emotions. By the time he got to his room, he was back in control.

That was close. What was he doing? He didn't need the complication of Sloan in his life. Look where it had gotten him. Now was not the time to lose his head over a woman, especially one he couldn't fully trust.

He pulled the white shirt from his bag, along with the pair of black jeans that would have to do for dress slacks. Finding his dark blazer, he slipped it on, and decided to hide his passport and money in a separate place in the room.

He secured them inside the lining of the ironing board, then checked his appearance in the mirror, pulling the mask of cold indifference onto his face. Satisfied at his success, he took his time heading back to Sloan's door and knocked.

She pulled it open and smiled, but one look at his cold expression drained the warmth from her eyes. As she beckoned him inside, he found Noah sitting on the chair in front of the little side desk, with censure in his gaze.

The tension in the room crackled, and he knew that Noah had probably said something disparaging about him. He must have chewed Sloan out as well. Wasn't that why she had a partner in the first place? Because she'd gone rogue one too many times, and Ramos was the person they blamed? And now, here he was again.

Sloan handed Ramos his ID badge. She had changed into a skirt and blouse, with her hair pulled back into a low ponytail. She slipped a pair of glasses onto her nose, and he couldn't help but compare them to the glasses Shelby wore when she first attended Manetto's meetings.

Right now, Ramos wished he was back home. His job with Manetto, and keeping Shelby alive, was a lot less complicated than being here in Cuba with Sloan.

Noah went over the plan with them again, and Ramos realized that Sloan and Noah had been working it out far longer than he'd realized. They even had a backup plan in case anything went wrong. From their preparation, he could see that the odds were much better for Sloan with his help, and that was enough to keep him in the mix. Still, he'd be glad when it was over.

Ramos glanced at the blueprint to set it in his mind, then checked his watch. "It's time to go."

Chapter 13

Sloan slung a purse across her shoulder, and Ramos followed her out of the hotel. Since the building wasn't far, they had decided to walk. Noah wasn't too far behind, and he followed them at a distance. His part in the plan consisted of keeping watch from across the street, and being ready to back them up or create a diversion if they needed it.

It surprised Ramos that they'd planned to communicate with texts rather than using high-end ear pieces, but Sloan had explained that their mission wasn't so big as to warrant all that spy-ware.

Nearly there, Sloan glanced at Ramos. "I hope you're not sorry I got you into this."

Ramos huffed. "I'll let you know when it's over." He caught her gaze. "What did Noah say after I left?" Sloan shook her head and pursed her lips, but didn't respond. It put Ramos on the defense. "Did he threaten you?"

She sighed. "He's not going to report me or anything. As long as we accomplish the mission, he's willing to keep his mouth shut. In fact, I've convinced him to leave you out of the narrative."

"How did you manage that?"

"Well, after destroying all of our weapons in Mexico, I'm sort of on probation with the department. Another slip-up and I'll be back at a desk job. Noah's a good guy, and he wants this to work, so I can count on him to keep his mouth shut. But, if I mess this up, he won't be able to. Know what I mean?"

Ramos sighed. "Yeah, I think so."

She turned to him with a desperate gleam in her eyes. "That's why I've got to succeed. I'm really hoping that I can get my hands on the device. Wouldn't that be something? I could solve this whole thing. It would boost my career and open a lot doors." She placed her hand on his arm. "That's why I'm grateful you're here. With your help, I'm sure we can pull it off."

Ramos nodded, but his brows rose in surprise at how much she was counting on him.

"I know we can do it," she said, mistaking his surprise for uncertainty. "You know how to take care of yourself. It makes a difference."

Ramos figured she was referring to their time in Mexico. He had a contingency plan that had saved their lives back then. Was she thinking he had something like that now? That was too bad, because he didn't have a damn thing to fall back on. A chill ran down his spine. What was he doing? So much could go wrong.

She smiled at him, her gaze hopeful. "After this is over, I'll make it up to you. I can take some time off. If we have to leave Cuba in a hurry, we can meet up in Miami. That might be better anyway."

Ramos let out a breath. She kept using that same old promise. So far, it seemed more like a one-way street. Of course, she had given him the information about his father.

He'd met an aunt and cousin that he didn't know he had. Still, he wasn't sure it was enough.

Then there was Sloan. He cared about her. More than he should. But he knew there could never be anything more between them, and he needed to let her go. "How about this," he said, wanting to save her feelings. "Let's get this job done. When it's over, we'll go from there."

She caught his gaze and smiled. "I'd like that." The vulnerability he'd seen in her eyes vanished, and she tilted her chin in the determined angle he was used to. He smiled back. He had no intention of leading her along, but now was not the time to talk about their relationship.

Coming closer to the building, they slowed their steps. With a quick adjustment, Ramos pulled his ID badge from the inside of his shirt, and Sloan did the same. Ready to put the plan into action, they walked the last few yards to the front of the building.

This mansion was old, a lot like the mansions in The Vedado section of the city, but this one was well maintained. The tall columns and upward staircase to the main doors reminded Ramos of classic Roman architecture.

As they climbed the stairs to the doors, they deliberately relaxed their shoulders to blend in, and spoke in Spanish about the weather and other mundane things.

Inside, an atrium with a glass chandelier opened up above them. Thick columns supported the oval space, and marble covered the floor. A staircase on the left led to the upper and lower floors. A few people were visible walking along the upper balcony between offices, but there wasn't a front desk with a receptionist. Instead, a man dressed in a uniform sat at a desk in the far right corner.

He cast a casual glance at them, but they ignored him and turned toward the staircase with deliberate steps, like they knew what they were doing, and started down. At the bottom, the hallway continued forward, with another going off to the right. From the blueprint, Ramos knew they met in a square shape with rooms opening up on either side.

The room they wanted was in the opposite corner from where they were, so they continued through the hallway, then turned right at the juncture. This part of the building seemed deserted, and every door they passed had a card reader in front of it.

Hoping their luck held, they continued to the end of the hall where the door they wanted waited at the end. As they reached the door, voices sounded from the direction they'd come. Ramos quickly pressed his badge to the reader and held his breath. The flashing light went from red to green, and he twisted the knob to open the door.

They hurried inside, and Ramos closed the door as softly as he could. Sloan flipped on the light, revealing an armory of some sort in front of them. The room was no larger than twenty by thirty feet. A cage-like fence, with a padlock and chain around the gated door, separated them from the large cache of weapons on the other side.

Inside the cage, one wall was lined with metal shelves housing rows of AK-47s. Another held several handguns and boxes of ammunition. Along the back wall were a few black cases that Ramos knew could hold just about anything.

"Can you see what we might be looking for in there?" Ramos whispered.

Sloan set her bag on the ground and opened it up. "We'll have to get inside for a better look." She pulled her lock-pick set out of the bag and froze. The handle on the door behind them wiggled, and they heard muffled voices. Ramos pulled Sloan to the other side of the door and switched off the light.

The handle jiggled once more, then the voices retreated. Ramos let out his breath and flipped the light back on. "We need to hurry."

Sloan nodded and handed him the picks. "Here, you do it. I'm not as good under pressure."

He took the set and examined the lock, then chose the right pick. A few seconds later, the lock snapped open. He uncoiled the chain and pulled the gate open. It let out a loud squeak that stopped his breath. Swallowing, he coaxed it open the rest of the way with hardly a sound, and they both stepped inside.

"It's got to be in one of these black cases," Sloan said.

Ramos grabbed a case and popped it open. Inside, rested a device that looked like a gun, but had a large speaker at the end of the barrel. Along the barrel were several round casings that connected together in a sophisticated sheath. A meter on one side showed a graph of numbers which ranged from zero to fifty-thousand.

"That's it," Sloan murmured breathlessly. She reached in and pulled the weapon out of the case. "I think it will fit in my bag." She opened her purse and settled it inside. "Let's get out of here."

"Wait," Ramos said, popping open another case. Just as he thought, another weapon lay inside. "It looks like we hit the jackpot." He counted eight cases, but Sloan had already left the enclosure. He quickly moved the empty case to the back, hoping it wouldn't be found anytime soon.

Sloan reached the door and glanced back at Ramos. "I'll get a head start. You cover me." She pulled the door open and rushed out.

Swearing under his breath, Ramos closed the gate and quickly pulled the chain together. He clicked the lock in place and hurried to the door. Turning out the light, he pulled it open and stepped into the hall. At the far end, he caught a glimpse of Sloan rounding the corner.

As he followed her, loud voices came from behind him, and he stepped up the pace. Just as he made it to the corner, a voice called out, ordering him to stop. Ahead of him, Sloan took off up the long staircase.

He knew he could make a run for it and catch up to her, but it would give her away, and they'd both get caught. Letting out a breath, he stopped and turned to face them, hoping he could bluff his way out.

"Si?" Ramos asked, stepping toward them so they wouldn't see Sloan's retreating figure.

The two men wore guard uniforms and carried guns. They spoke in rapid Spanish and asked what he was doing down there. He held up his badge and answered that he worked there.

The man's brows drew together with suspicion, and Ramos worried that he'd said the wrong thing. Questioning him further, one guard asked him what room he'd been in, and Ramos pointed to the room at the end of the hall. The guard motioned him in that direction, and Ramos shrugged, then walked back that way.

By the time they reached the door, Ramos hoped he'd given Sloan enough time to leave the building, because he was ready to make his move. He held his ID badge over the card reader. The light turned green, and he pushed the door open, flipping on the light so they could see inside. He held the door open and invited them to take a look, claiming that he'd been sent to check on the inventory.

As one of the guards glanced inside, Ramos shoved his head against the doorframe, then pushed him into the room. Caught by surprise, the other guard reached for his gun, but Ramos landed a punch that knocked him sideways.

Ramos quickly shoved him inside the room, slamming the door behind him. With a well-placed kick to the first man, and an elbow to the jaw of the second, it didn't take long before they were both lying half-unconscious on the floor. Breathing heavily, Ramos turned out the light and stepped outside into the hall.

This time, he ran down the hall. As he rounded the corner, three guards stood waiting for him with their guns drawn. He slid to a stop and quickly lifted his arms in surrender. The leader shouted at him to lie down face-first on the floor. He did as he was told and soon found his arms cuffed behind him.

As they dragged him to his feet, the other guards he'd left behind staggered into the hall. They told the officer in charge what Ramos had done to them, and in which room they'd been left. The officer pulled Ramos's ID badge from around his neck and began questioning him, but Ramos kept his mouth shut.

In growing frustration, the head guard commanded that they take Ramos away. As they marched him up the stairs, he picked up that they planned to take him to the Villa Marista for further questioning. His heart began to pound, and his breath caught.

Just a couple of hours ago he had driven by that place, and now they were taking him back there? This just got a whole lot worse. His heart sank. How was he going to get out of this one?

As the guards escorted him outside to their Russian-made car, he glanced up and down the street, hoping for a glimpse of Noah or Sloan, so they'd know he'd been taken. He didn't spot either of them, and his breath caught with despair. What could they do anyway? He wasn't one of them. They couldn't help him. He was on his own.

Shoving him into the back seat, the two guards got in the front and began the drive through Havana to the outskirts of town. Sinister foreboding washed over him, and Ramos kept his gaze on the blue sky and puffy white clouds, taking in what he worried could be his last sight of freedom.

All too soon, the car pulled into the drive of the square, block-shaped building, and stopped in front of the guardhouse. After exchanging a few words, the guard pulled the gate open to allow the car to enter.

After parking, the driver opened Ramos's door and prodded him out. Flanked by both guards holding his arms with a firm grip, they took Ramos inside a set of double-doors, through a security checkpoint, and marched him down an ugly, green-painted corridor to a room with an old vinyl couch and buzzing fluorescent lights. They pushed Ramos down on a rough, wooden bench that was hammered into the wall, and moved toward a high desk at the other end of the room.

Behind the desk, a dirty glass window opened up into a control room. An old man with a pot belly, who was smoking a cigar, stepped out of the room. The guards joined him, but they didn't speak loudly enough for Ramos to hear what they said.

A moment later, the guards came back to Ramos and pulled him up. They marched him down another hall into a small room. The old man followed, carrying a wooden club. He slapped it against his palm like he couldn't wait to use it, and Ramos tensed.

Inside the room, a desk sat in the center with chairs on both sides. While one guard held Ramos's arm, the other guard unlocked his handcuffs. As they brought his arms together in front of him, the old man stood ready for any excuse to use the club, keeping Ramos in check.

The handcuffs clicked into place on his wrists, and they pushed him into the chair, locking the cuffs into a chain bolted on the table. Finished, all three of them left the room, and Ramos had a moment to catch his breath.

How had this happened? He could hardly believe where he was. The irony would have made him laugh if it wasn't so dire. The officer who'd caught him in the building entered the room with a sneer. Ramos sat up straight and sent him a pointed look of his own. "This is a mistake," he said in Spanish.

"We know you are not Ramon Pérez like it says on your ID badge," the man answered in Spanish. "You know what goes on here, so I will make it easy for you. If you want to survive, there are two things you must do. Tell us your name, and tell us what you were doing in that room."

Ramos weighed his options before he spoke, this time in English. "My name is Rafael Ramirez. And I'll be happy to speak with the person responsible for the sonic device you've been using to attack the United States."

The officer's eyes widened with surprise, and Ramos caught a sliver of alarm that bolstered his courage. The officer covered his alarm by blustering that Ramos didn't know what he was talking about. Ramos refused to be baited and kept his mouth shut.

The officer scowled and shook his head. "We'll see how silent you are when General Zarco gets here." He abruptly stood and hurried out of the room.

Ramos let out his breath and closed his eyes. It was a big gamble to mention the sonic device, but it was the only leverage he had, and he wasn't going down without a fight. Using his father's name had been an impulse, but since he was in the place where his father had most likely been held, it seemed appropriate.

There wasn't a two-way mirror in this room, but he spotted a camera in the corner directed his way and figured they were watching him. At least they hadn't taken his clothes and his phone. That was to his advantage, since he still had the lock-pick in his jacket pocket. But, with his hands secured to the table, there wasn't a way he could reach them. Still, it gave him hope that he had something to use to escape.

Time passed slowly, and Ramos grew uncomfortable in the hard chair. He glanced up at the camera and noticed that there wasn't a red light, indicating that the camera had power. Did that mean it wasn't working?

Deciding to take a chance, he shifted his weight to see if he could lean far enough over his hands to reach the lock pick in his jacket. That didn't work, so he tried to use his arm to push his jacket closer to his mouth. If he could get his mouth close enough to the pocket, he might be able to grab the lock pick between his lips.

After several failures, he almost had it when footsteps sounded in the hall. Just as he straightened, the door flew open, and an older man wearing a general's uniform entered the room. This had to be Zarco. He was average height and older than Ramos had imagined, but he stood tall with authority. Zarco took one look at Ramos and jerked to a stop. His eyes widened with surprise and a touch of fear. "You? It's not possible."

A guard had followed him into the room, but Zarco turned toward the guard and told him to get out and close the door. The guard hesitated, but did as he was commanded, shutting the door and sending the lock home.

It wasn't much, but it had given Zarco enough time to compose himself, and his gaze held more reserve than before. He stepped to the chair across from Ramos and sat down, studying Ramos carefully before shaking his head.

"You look just like him," he began. "But I know it can't be true because Rafael is dead. I made sure of that."

Ramos's breath caught with surprise. This was the man who had killed his father? He'd thought it was Vincente. Of course, Zarco could have ordered Rafael's death, and Vincente could have been the one who'd killed him.

Ramos did his best to hold his emotions in check, not wanting this man to know how his confession affected him. He also knew that Zarco was probably baiting him with his boast, and Ramos wasn't about to give him the satisfaction of a reaction.

Then Ramos decided a different course of action was warranted. He narrowed his gaze and shook his head. "I always suspected it was you." He paused, wanting to throw him off. "Does your government know you're plotting with the Russians?" Zarco's gaze flicked with unease, giving Ramos a small hope, that if he was acting alone, Ramos could use this against him.

"Rafael was a traitor," Zarco said, changing the subject. "He had no honor. Who are you to him?"

Ramos wasn't about to answer that question. "A terrorist attack against the United States is an act of war. Is that what you want?"

"We have done no such thing."

A knock sounded at the door, and the general let out a sigh before standing. At the door, the guard spoke quietly to him. Zarco cursed and glanced at Ramos before rushing to the table. This time he loomed over Ramos with fire in his eyes.

"Where is it? What have you done with it?"

Ramos kept his mouth shut, but didn't lower his gaze. He stared Zarco down while Zarco opened and closed his mouth. Then, slapping his hands against the table, Zarco roared in rage that Ramos was an idiot, calling him names and venting his anger.

Finally out of breath, he stopped shouting, and inhaled several times to pull himself together. "You won't talk now. But you will soon enough. You are not the first American spy we have captured. With the right motivation, you will give up your secrets just like all the rest." Zarco straightened and leveled an intimidating stare at Ramos.

It had just the opposite effect. Ramos let out a chuckle and shook his head. "That's the irony of this whole thing. I'm not a spy."

Zarco sneered. "Then it won't matter if I kill you." He left the room, shutting the door loudly behind him.

Chapter 14

Ramos didn't have long to wait before the guards returned, along with the old man and his club. They cuffed his hands behind him and led him down another corridor, then into the dark recesses of the building. The dirty gray walls smelled of mold and sweat. Every so often, Ramos could hear the sounds of inmates talking, but even that soon disappeared.

They passed through another gated security checkpoint, and Ramos despaired of ever getting out of there. This corridor continued further into the bowels of the building. With the fluorescent lights blinking in and out, the smells got worse, and there wasn't a sign of life anywhere.

As they walked, their footfalls echoed down the corridor, and it seemed to Ramos that his life was getting snuffed out one step at a time. He'd be left to rot in this hellhole, and no one would ever know what had happened to him.

Was this what had happened to his father? He should have listened to his Aunt Rosalyn, and Vincente's wife. Why had he ever come? Because of Sloan. He had lowered his guard and come to care for her. Never again. If he ever got out of this, he swore that the only people he would allow to get close to him was the family he already had with Manetto, Shelby, and only those he trusted.

At last, the guards stopped in front of a door at the end of the long hall. Pulling a set of keys from his pocket, the guard unlocked the door and turned on the inside light. The musty odor of blood and decay filled Ramos's nostrils, sending a shiver of dread down his spine.

A long table rested at the back wall of the room, with several instruments of torture lying on top of it. One side of the room held a single chair with opened locks on the arms and legs. On the other side, chains with cuffs on the ends hung from the ceiling.

The guards roughly propelled Ramos toward the chair, and panic clawed into his chest. Without thought for the consequences, he struggled against them, but the old man following raised his club.

A sharp pain exploded across the back of Ramos's head, and he slumped, dazed from the blow. The guards thrust him into the chair, unbound his cuffs, and quickly snapped the locks around his wrists and ankles. After checking his locks one more time, they left the room.

Pain radiated down Ramos's neck, and he took deep breaths to keep from throwing up. Several minutes later, the pain began to lessen, and the nausea passed. He closed his eyes and tried to come up with a plan to get out of there.

If they thought he was a spy, there might be a chance they'd let him live. Too bad he'd said he wasn't. He hadn't seen Sloan on the street, but there was a possibility she'd seen them haul him out. Would she try to get him out of there?

He huffed out a breath. Probably not, since she went against the agency to have his help in the first place. Unless she tried something on her own, he couldn't expect help from her or the agency she worked for.

Was there anyone else who would help him? No. Not a single person. And, by using his father's name, he may have just put his aunt and cousin in jeopardy. So what should he do? There was still the angle that Zarco was working without the Cuban government's knowledge. Maybe he could use that and see where it got him.

The door rattled, and Zarco stepped inside. He came in alone and quickly closed the door behind him. He glanced dispassionately at Ramos, then stepped behind him to the table with the instruments. Hearing the sounds of Zarco sorting through the tools sent cold fear into Ramos's chest.

"As you know, one of my sonic weapons is missing. I know you were working with someone. I want to know who it is, and where I can find them."

Zarco stepped in front of Ramos and dispassionately unbuttoned Ramos's shirt, pulling it out of the way to expose his bare chest. Standing this close, Zarco reeked of tobacco. With his lips tightly pressed together, Zarco inhaled through his nostrils. His breath whistled in and out of his nose like a bull getting ready to charge.

Then he was done, and he moved back to the table, giving Ramos a moment to catch his breath. A sudden urge to pull at the manacles came over him, but he resisted the inclination and concentrated on breathing deeply to stay calm.

He heard the flip of a switch, and a low, humming sound echoed through the room. His stomach clenched, and the muscles in his shoulders and neck tightened. A moment later, Zarco stepped into Ramos's view, wearing rubber gloves, and holding an electrical device in each hand.

He stood in front of Ramos. "Ready to talk?" He waited for Ramos to speak but, when he didn't, Zarco shook his head. "I've heard this is quite painful. I usually start at a low voltage and work my way up, but for you I'm afraid I don't have time for that. Are you sure you have nothing to say?"

Ramos swallowed but kept his mouth shut.

"Try not to bite off your tongue." Zarco lowered the buzzing cables slowly toward Ramos's chest. Anticipation glowed in his eyes, and Ramos braced himself.

Suddenly, the door burst open. Zarco spun toward the intruder with a growl. Ramos's eyes widened with surprise to find Vincente Garcia standing in the doorway.

"General. Excuse the intrusion, but I must speak with you."

"Can't it wait?"

"Perhaps." Vincente stepped inside and closed the door. "Who is this?"

Zarco sighed, then took a step back and shook his head. "He said his name is Rafael Ramirez, but we both know that isn't true."

"Sí, we do. What has this man done? Perhaps I can help?"

Surprise rippled through Ramos. Why was Vincente putting on an act?

"This is military business," Zarco said, puffing up his chest with authority. "It doesn't concern you."

Vincente nodded. "I see. Forgive me. The truth is...when I heard you had arrested a man with the name of Rafael Ramirez...well, I was curious."

Zarco relaxed his stance and gave Vincente a nod. "Yes. Of course."

"And I wanted to see him." Vincente stepped closer to examine Ramos. "There is a resemblance, isn't there?" Zarco nodded, and Vincente continued. "I also heard that he was caught in the defense ministry building. Why would he go there?"

Zarco glanced at Vincente with narrowed eyes. "He managed to get inside an off-limits storage room, and he took something that he shouldn't have. He didn't have the item with him, so I know he was working with someone else. I'm trying to persuade him to tell me everything he knows about it."

"Do you think he's an American spy?" Vincente asked, arching his brow.

"Yes," Zarco answered, then seemed to realize he had spoken too quickly. "We are wasting time. I need to find out where the item is."

Ramos had heard enough. "It's a sonic weapon that he's using against the American diplomats. The one everyone's talking about."

Zarco sucked in a breath. "Shut up!" He slapped the cables onto Ramos's bare chest and pushed the buttons. Pain shot across his body, and he stifled a scream. His back arched upward from the shock, and his muscles clenched. The jolt stopped his breath, rippling through his body in horrific waves of agony. Just as he thought his heart would give out, the excruciating torment stopped, and he fell back against the chair.

Heaving in labored breaths, Ramos opened his eyes to find Zarco knocked to the ground, with Vincente standing over him. Vincente grabbed the dangling cables, shoved them down onto Zarco's chest, and pushed the buttons. Zarco's scream pierced the air, and his body jerked with spasms.

Ramos swallowed down his nausea, and tried to make sense of what he was seeing. Vincente held the cables down on Zarco's chest for what seemed like hours. He didn't let up until Zarco's screaming stopped, and his eyes had rolled back into his head.

Finally, Vincente pulled the cables away and sat back on his heels. Breathing heavily, he got to his feet and replaced the cables on the table where they belonged. Then he knelt down on one knee and felt Zarco's neck for a pulse.

"He's dead." Vincente glanced at Ramos, then let out a breath and stood. He took a handkerchief from his back pocket and wiped his sweating face. Replacing the handkerchief, he moved to the table and found the keys to Ramos's manacles. At Ramos's side, he swiftly unlocked the manacles at his wrists and ankles.

Ramos rubbed his wrists, relieved, but swimming in confusion. "Why did you do that?"

Vincente shook his head, and a grimace of disgust twisted his lips. "I will explain. But first, I need to get you out of here so that I can take care of this mess." He motioned to the dead general. "I think I can do it, but I need you to tell me exactly what happened and what you found."

Ramos told him about the sonic devices, how many there were, and what they looked like. "The American agents managed to take one. As far as I know, they still have it."

Vincente sucked in a breath, then glanced at Ramos. "And they left you behind? Are they coming back for you?"

Ramos's lips turned up in a sardonic twist. "I doubt it. Conveniently for them, I'm not part of their group. It's a long story, but I'm not a spy. I work for a mob-boss, so I've crossed paths with them a few times."

Vincente's eyes widened with surprise, then narrowed with comprehension. "I see. They have something on you. Well, it is no matter. I know what to do now." He glanced at Zarco and let out a breath. "I've wanted to kill him for a long time."

He caught Ramos's gaze, and his lips tightened into a grim line, then he stepped back to the table and grabbed the handcuffs. "Before we leave, I have to put the cuffs back on you, but don't worry, no one will question me. I will get you out."

Ramos nodded and stood. His legs shook, and his vision swam, but he took a breath and held still until everything came back into focus. With shaking hands, he buttoned up his shirt and tucked it back into his pants. "Okay. I'm ready."

Vincente pulled Ramos's arms behind him and locked the cuffs, then took hold of his arm and waited for Ramos to take a step. His first steps were a little unsteady but, with Vincente's help, Ramos soon regained his footing, and they made it to the door.

Ramos waited while Vincente opened the door, then stepped through, surprised to find the hall empty. Vincente locked the door behind them and took Ramos's arm. Ramos wasn't sure if it was to steady him, or to make it look official, but he was grateful for Vincente's firm grip.

Shaky, and with his nerves on edge, the walk out seemed longer than the walk in. At the checkpoint, the guard acknowledged Vincente and opened the gate without a word. A few minutes later, they rounded the corner to the first room Ramos had been taken to.

The old man who'd clubbed Ramos over the head nodded at Vincente, then moved to take the lead. He cleared the way for Vincente and Ramos to reach the last checkpoint before the exit.

The officer who'd caught Ramos at the defense building stood just inside the doors. His gaze widened with alarm to see Ramos with Vincente, and he stepped forward to stop them. "What are you doing? He cannot leave."

Vincente glanced at the officer with distaste, then motioned to the old man. "Take him."

He moved quickly, for an old guy, and soon had the guard in hand. The officer protested but, under Vincente's pointed gaze, he closed his mouth and quit struggling.

Vincente nodded his approval. "Good. You learn fast. I will take care of this one way or another. Cooperate with me and you will live. Understand?" At his nod, Vincente continued. "We will clear this up. Sí?" The officer nodded with comprehension and relief. "Good. I'll be back shortly."

Vincente glanced at the old man with an unspoken command, and the old man led the officer away. At the last checkpoint before exiting the building, Vincente called ahead to the guards, telling them to bring his car around.

Barely a minute later, a Toyota Land Cruiser pulled up. The guards opened the last double-doors, and Ramos walked out of the prison with Vincente. The sun had set, and the sky was darkening, but it was a beautiful sight, and Ramos took a deep breath of fresh air.

The driver came around and opened the back door. Vincente helped Ramos inside, and Ramos slid across the seat to allow Vincente to sit beside him. The driver pulled away from the building, then slowed at the outer gates. The guards stationed there quickly pushed the gates open, and the driver pulled through. Before turning onto the street, Vincente told the driver to take them to Ramos's hotel.

"Turn around," Vincente said to Ramos. He quickly unlocked Ramos's cuffs, then sat back in his seat. "As you can imagine, I have some things to take care of, but if you could come to my home around ten tonight, I will explain."

Ramos rubbed his wrists, still a little dazed that he'd made it out of that place alive. He owed Vincente his life. "Yes. Of course. I'll be there."

"Good. You should also make arrangements to leave Cuba...tomorrow."

Ramos nodded. "I will."

"I must also warn you that we are still looking for your associates. If we find them, they will be shown no mercy."

"I understand." It was easy to see that the same rules for helping Ramos didn't apply to Sloan and Noah. Ramos had no idea what had happened to them, but he hoped they were long gone.

Weary, and suddenly thirsty, Ramos closed his eyes against the pounding in his skull. He touched the back of his head to find a lump, but at least the skin wasn't broken. He needed some aspirin and a drink. Some food would be nice, too. But, after everything that had happened, he was incredibly grateful to be alive.

The car pulled up in front of his hotel, and Ramos got out. He glanced at Vincente and nodded his thanks before closing the door. As the car drove away, he heard Vincente telling his driver where to go next. He didn't envy the mess Vincente had to clean up, and wondered how he'd pull it off. What if he couldn't? Would the soldiers come back to get him?

He took the elevator to the third floor and shuffled to his room. Using the keycard to unlock the door, he flipped on the light. After filling a glass with water and drinking it down, he dug his cell phone from his pocket and switched it on.

He'd missed three phone calls, all from Sloan. He pulled up his voice mail and listened to each one. In the first, Sloan sounded breathless and frightened. "Ramos! I saw them take you. I'm not going to leave you behind. I'll do everything I can to get you out of there."

The second was more controlled, but harder to hear because of the sounds of an engine and heavy wind in the background. "We had to leave. Wells sent a team after us, but I'll try and come back. I promise. I'll do everything I can."

In the third message, her remorse and guilt came through in waves. "Ramos...I know you'll probably never hear this. But...I need you to know that I never meant for this to happen. I shouldn't have involved you with any of this. I'm so sorry. This is all my fault. I don't know if I can get you out, but I'll do what I can. I'll never stop trying to find you. I promise. I'm so sorry."

He sank down in the chair and closed his eyes. At least they'd made it out of there, so he didn't have to worry about that. The precariousness of the whole situation hit him like a ton of bricks. Without Vincente's intervention, he'd be dead.

Helping Sloan was the stupidest thing he'd ever done. He could never put himself in that position again. It didn't matter how much he cared for her, or what she promised him, or how she felt. He was done with having her in his life.

He let out a sigh and pushed her number.

"Ramos?"

"It's me."

She let out a relieved breath. "Are you okay?"

"I'm fine." He heard someone speaking to Sloan, so he waited until she came back on the line.

"Are they asking for something?" she asked. "Like money, or the device?"

"Uh...no. I got out. They let me go."

Sloan gasped. "What? They let you go? I never thought..."

"I have to leave tomorrow, but I just wanted you to know I'm okay."

"How did you get out?"

"It's a long story." He wasn't about to explain anything over the phone, especially when he knew someone was there and most likely listening to the conversation.

"Okay, sure. Wow. I can hardly believe it. I can't tell you how relieved I am. So you're flying out tomorrow?"

"That's the plan. I'll call you when I get to Miami. We'll talk then."

"Okay. Call me the minute you land. All right?"

"I'll call you tomorrow, Sloan." He disconnected and set his phone on the table. Rubbing his face, he let out a breath. What a mess this was. Now he had to worry about who was listening, and if she'd told her superiors that he'd been involved with the whole thing. How would that affect him?

With a sigh, he stood, then pulled off his jacket and unbuttoned his shirt. He needed a shower to wash the stink of that place from his body and mind. Catching sight of his bare chest in the mirror, he found two red burns like round suction cups on his skin.

Just the memory of that pain sent a shiver through him. He turned on the hot water and stood beneath the spray for a good ten minutes before he felt better. Finishing up, he toweled dry and got dressed. Hunger and thirst drove him from his room, but at least he wasn't shaking anymore.

He stopped at the front desk and asked for the concierge. A woman emerged from the back office and smiled at him. "What can I do for you?"

"I need to book a flight to Miami tomorrow. Can you help me with that?"

"Of course." She pulled up the information on her computer. There were only two seats left on the morning flight at ten-thirty. She told him there was another flight with more room in the afternoon, if he wanted to wait. Ramos wasn't about to take any chances and told her to book one of the earlier seats. As she got to work, he hardly dared to breathe until his flight was confirmed.

She printed out his boarding pass, and he took it with relief. After stowing it away in his wallet, he asked about a good restaurant nearby. She pointed him to the one across the street, and he thanked her. Leaving the hotel, he made his way to the restaurant, hoping to blend in with the other tourists. He didn't notice anyone taking a special interest in him and was grateful to sit down at a table where he didn't feel cornered.

He took note of all the exits and kept an eye on the people around him. After several minutes, he found nothing out of place, and finally glanced over his menu. The waiter took his order, and it wasn't long before the arroz con pollo was placed in front of him.

It smelled delicious, and Ramos began to eat. He glanced up every so often, vigilantly watching for an attack. Soon the food lost its flavor, because he couldn't shake the worry that, at any moment, a military guard or a police officer would walk in and arrest him. Even a famous Cuban Mojito did little to curb his anxiety. It did take the edge off, and he finally finished his dinner.

At nine-forty, he paid his bill and found a taxi. He arrived at Vincente's house a little early, but Yanara's welcoming smile put him at ease.

"Vincente is upstairs, but he'll be down in a minute. Can I get you something? I made torticas de moron, uh...sugar cookies. Would you like one?"

"Sure. Thanks."

He sat back in the chair and closed his eyes, feeling safe for the first time since he'd been released from the prison. Yanara returned with a plate of cookies and set them on the coffee table. He took one and ate it, surprised at the lime and rum flavoring. "This is really good. Thanks."

He was on his second cookie when Vincente entered the room. Vincente's hair was wet from a shower, and he carried a weight on his shoulders that hadn't been there before. With his entrance, Yanara announced that she was going to bed and bid them goodnight. "Don't stay up too late," she admonished her husband.

He nodded absently and walked to the liquor cabinet. He pulled out a bottle of rum and two glasses. After setting them on the table, he poured a splash into each glass and set the bottle down. He took a sip before turning to Ramos. "This has been an interesting day."

Ramos nodded his agreement and waited for Vincente to begin.

"When are you leaving?" Vincente asked.

"Tomorrow morning."

"Good, good." Vincente took another swallow and leaned back into his chair. "And your friends? Do you know what happened to them?"

"They left. I'm certain they're back in the states...with the device."

Vincente took a deep breath and shook his head. "Zarco had too much power, and he hated anything to do with the states. He didn't want better relations between the countries, which drove him to make the attacks. It seems to have worked, but that is my problem...Cuba's problem now."

He studied Ramos, then took another swallow of his drink before he began. "I'm sure you are wondering why I stepped in to help you. It was true when I told you that your father and I were good friends. He was an idealist. It got him into trouble. I was not a believer in rocking the boat, so we didn't always agree. But when I found out that he was about to be arrested, I'm the one who warned him. I also helped him get out of Cuba."

Vincente swirled the rum in his glass, but his gaze was far away. "He got you and your family out in time, so I was dismayed to learn that he'd been captured and was being held in the Villa Marista. General Zarco was only a commander then, but he had made it his mission to bring down the dissenters in a bid to prove himself to the regime and move up in the ranks.

"Zarco wanted the names of everyone in Rafael's organization. He especially wanted the name of the person who had helped him escape Cuba. But Rafael refused to tell him."

Vincente glanced at Ramos with eyes that held pain and sorrow. "Zarco called me into the interrogation room, and I saw what he had done to Rafael. The poor man was barely alive. Seeing him like that, and knowing he hadn't turned me in..." He made a fist and shook his head. "He saved my life, but it tore me up inside."

Vincente took a breath to control his emotions, then his voice turned hard and cold. "Zarco complained to me that Rafael hadn't given him anything. He'd done everything he could think of to get him to talk, even threatening his family, but Rafael never broke. Then Zarco looked at me, and dark calculation filled his eyes. He knew we'd been friends so, to prove my loyalty, he gave me the task of ending Rafael's life."

Ramos shook his head. Anger burned inside of him, and he wished Zarco wasn't dead so he could be the one to kill him. He glanced at Vincente, knowing he'd paid a terrible price for his high position in the government, but Ramos couldn't judge him. Not now. "Did you do it?"

Vincente's stark gaze didn't waver from his, and Ramos braced himself for the truth. "I told Zarco I would kill him, but I asked for some time to see if I could get Rafael to talk to me. I explained that he might talk to an old friend and confess everything.

"Zarco liked that idea and quickly agreed. But, with Rafael so close to death, I needed some time to bring him around. It worked as I'd hoped, and Zarco went home for the night, leaving me alone with Rafael, saying he'd be back in the morning.

"As soon as Zarco left, I lowered Rafael's battered body to the ground and unlocked the chains from his wrists and ankles. I gave him water and bathed his bruised and swollen face. I did what I could to make him comfortable.

"It was near dawn when he opened his eyes. He could hardly speak. I told him what Zarco wanted me to do. He whispered that he was okay with dying, as long as I promised to make sure his family was safe. I'll never forget the look in his eyes as he held on to life, waiting for my response. The moment I agreed, his body relaxed, and he died in my arms."

Ramos's eyes glazed over with unshed tears. He'd been in the exact same room where his father had died. But at least Rafael hadn't died alone. Vincente was there, like a true friend.

"Zarco was disappointed that Rafael had died before he'd told me anything, and I think he always had his doubts about me. But there was nothing he could do about it. I did what I could to fulfill my promise and sent word to a friend in the states to make sure your family was out of danger.

"I also steered retaliation away from Rafael's family here in Cuba. This home belonged to your mother's family. They took the brunt of the harassment, and I persuaded them to move away before things got worse. I got their home, and they managed to get enough money to leave Cuba for good."

Vincente closed his eyes and let out a breath. "Then you came. I knew who you were the moment I saw you. I wanted to tell you that Rafael was dead, but I thought it best to encourage you to leave it alone. It happened a long time ago, and I didn't want to bring unwanted attention your way or mine. Since you used a different name, I didn't think you'd be in danger here.

"In fact, the only danger I could sense was that you were here to kill the man responsible for your father's death." He grimaced. "I even wondered if you'd come after me. That's why I asked Yanara to give you the few photos of your family that we'd kept. I'd hoped it would be enough to satisfy your curiosity."

He shook his head. "When my officer at the Villa Marista told me someone named Rafael Ramirez had been caught, I didn't know what to think. Then to learn that Zarco had come to interrogate him, I knew that I had to act quickly. It was a shock to find you in that room with Zarco...just like your father. I'm glad I got there in time to stop him."

"I'm glad that you killed him," Ramos said. "Will they come after you now?"

Vincente snorted. "No. Thanks to you, I have the evidence of Zarco's collusion with the Russians. It may have been sanctioned by one or two people in power, but the majority of the council would never support such an act. In the end, it will be made to look like he was acting on his own."

Ramos nodded. "And I can leave?"

"Yes," Vincente agreed. "Rafael Ramirez died a long time ago. If anyone is looking for him, it will come to nothing, but it was good you used his name. It protected you more than you know. And now Alejandro Ramos is free to go."

Ramos stood, suddenly weary to the bone. "Thank you Vincente. Thanks for keeping your promise to my father."

"He was a good, honorable man," Vincente said, standing. He held out his hand, and Ramos took it, then Vincente pulled him in close and clapped Ramos on the back. "It would probably be best if you never came back. I know you have family here but, for their safety..."

"I know. I won't be back," Ramos said, stepping away. "But, if you ever need me, don't hesitate to reach out. I'd be willing to help you any time." Ramos took a business card from his wallet and handed it to Vincente. "It's a secure number."

"Thank you, Alejandro. I hope I never have to, but it is good to have friends, sí?"

"Yes. Please tell Yanara thanks for everything."

"I will." Vincente opened the door, and Ramos walked out. A calming peace settled over him. It was over. At the gate, he glanced back. Vincente nodded at him, then closed the door.

Back at the hotel, he fell into bed, exhausted and sad about his father. At least he knew what had happened to him, and the man responsible for it was dead. Ramos would probably be dead too if Vincente hadn't kept his promise.

He also didn't have to worry about his aunt and cousin, which came as a huge relief. It was too bad that they believed Vincente was the man behind his father's death, rather than the one who had kept them safe all these years. But it didn't seem to bother Vincente, and Ramos could understand why. He figured that taking the blame for being the bad guy made it easier to be the good guy once in a while.

Chapter 15

Ramos stood in line at the airport, waiting to go through security. Even though his stomach clenched with nerves, he kept his expression and mannerisms calm. His turn came, and he handed the agent his passport and boarding pass.

The agent glanced at his screen, then frowned. He looked at Ramos and told him to step aside while he made a phone call. Ramos did as he was told, only showing mild irritation, but his heart began to pound, especially when an officer approached the agent.

He took Ramos's passport and glanced at him with narrowed eyes, then back at the passport before handing it back. "Sorry for the inconvenience, Señor Ramos. You are free to go. We hope you have enjoyed your stay."

Ramos didn't know if the officer was being sarcastic or serious, but he sent him a nod and took his passport, eager to continue to the gate. Waiting to board the plane seemed to take forever, and it wasn't until his plane left the ground that he could finally breathe again.

Landing in Miami unfurled the last of his anxiety, and he exited the plane with an extra spring in his step, grateful to make it home alive.

He rented his usual black sports car and drove back to the hotel where he'd stayed just a few days ago. He got a room and collected the bag he'd left, realizing that a lot had changed in those short few days. Now he had a heritage, and a connection to his own father, that he'd never thought possible.

Did it change the direction of his life? Not really, but knowing more about his father gave him a foundation he'd never had before. He pulled the curtains in his room open and gazed over the city at the blue skies, enjoying the view and the freedom it represented.

Then he pulled out his phone and put the call through to Sloan.

She picked up right away. "Ramos? Is that you?"

"Yeah. I'm in Miami."

She let out a big sigh. "Thank God. I was so worried. They took you and I...it was horrible. There was nothing I could do, and it was all my fault."

"It's okay, Sloan. I got out. I'm back in the states and I'm fine. So what happened on your end? How did you guys get back?"

"After you got caught, we knew they'd be looking for us, so we didn't dare go back to the hotel. Noah had a secondary location staked out, so we went there and called my boss. He sent a team in a helicopter to extract us. We didn't even get to go back to the hotel for our things." She let out a breath. "I told them I wasn't leaving without you, but they wouldn't let me stay."

"I'm glad you left. You couldn't have helped me."

"So what happened? How did you get out?"

"It's a long story." Ramos wasn't sure he wanted to get into it right then.

"I know...you already said that." Sloan waited a moment before continuing. "At least give me something."

"Vincente pulled some strings. Let's just say that he was once friends with my father, and he intervened because of that."

"Did he know what happened to your dad?"

"Yes," Ramos said. "He died a long time ago."

"Oh. I'm sorry." Sloan took a breath. "Um...I had to tell my boss you helped us, but he agreed to leave you out of the official report. It's the best I could do, but it should keep your name out of it."

Did she expect him to thank her? He wasn't about to do that. "Good."

"Yeah. Uh...I'm in Fort Lauderdale right now, but I should be able to get away tomorrow or the next day. Do you think you could stay until then? I'd like to hear the whole story, and I really want to see you."

Ramos closed his eyes. He wanted to see Sloan, too. Even after everything that had happened. But he couldn't be involved with her. That was insane. "I have something that I need to take care of," he said. "So...I think that will work."

"Great. I've got to go, but I'll call you soon."

They disconnected, and he sighed. What had he just done? Why had he agreed? He had no intention of continuing a relationship with her, and he needed to make it perfectly clear that he was never going to help her again.

He let out a breath. He could just leave, but maybe it was time to lay it all out. After she knew how he felt, he'd let her decide if she wanted to spend any more time with him. She could apologize all she wanted, but it wasn't going to change his mind.

Glad that was settled, he put a call through to Manetto, eager to hear a friendly voice.

"Ramos. It's good to hear from you," Manetto said. "How did things go?"

"Let's just say it's a long story, and I'm glad to be back in Miami."

"Hmm...I take it Sloan was involved?"

"Yeah, but at least I know what happened to my father, so it's all good. I have a couple of things to take care of while I'm here, so I thought I'd stay a few more days."

"That's not a problem," Manetto agreed. "I'm actually in Seattle right now helping Kate with some business. There's a couple of new contracts I needed to go over with her, but so far the Passinis have been good to work with, so take as much time as you need."

"You're with Kate? I'm not sure I like that."

"I'm fine. All of them are bending over backwards for me, so there's nothing to worry about."

"They'd better be," Ramos said, not sure he trusted them. Or was it Kate he didn't trust? Probably both. "I'll let you know when I'm done, but if you need me to come to Seattle, I will."

"Thanks, but I'm not worried."

"Okay, good. Oh...and I got you those cigars you wanted."

Manetto chuckled. "Thanks. And...since you're in Miami, I wouldn't mind if you wanted to stop by the club. It's always good to let them think I'm checking up on them. Maybe even play a few rounds of poker, but it's up to you."

Ramos smiled. "If you were Shelby, I'd say you'd read my mind, since that was my plan." They both laughed, and Ramos was suddenly grateful for the life he had. Sure it could have been different, but his life was good, and he didn't want it to change.

"And don't think you're off the hook," Manetto said. "Once things have settled down, I'd like to know exactly what happened in Cuba. All of it."

Ramos smiled. He hadn't confided in Manetto much, but it might be nice to tell him about his father. If there was anyone in the world who would understand what he'd just been through, it was Manetto. "Sure. I'll tell you all about it."

"Good. One more thing. I know I don't say it much, but I'm glad you're back."

"Thanks. Me too." They disconnected, and Ramos smiled, grateful to have Manetto on his side.

With renewed purpose, he spent the next hour going through the photos and letters that Yanara had given him. There were two letters that he hadn't taken the time to read, so he took them out and opened them. Both were from his mother to his father. They were filled with everyday news, and gave him a small sense of his parents' life in Cuba.

After reading them, a wave of melancholy swept over him. His parents had loved each other deeply, and had hoped for a wonderful life together that would never be. Glancing through the photos, he could picture what their lives had been like, something he'd never imagined until now.

He knew what he needed to do with the photos. His brother, Javier, lived in Miami, and Ramos wanted him to have them. Javier believed Ramos was dead, which was just the way Ramos wanted it. But that didn't mean he couldn't leave a large envelope, containing this small slice of their lives, on his doorstep. It also didn't hurt that he could get another look at his brother and his family from a distance.

He bought an envelope large enough to hold everything and wrote a short message on the outside. It took him a moment to figure out what to write, but he decided to keep it simple. He wrote: To Javier, Pictures of your parents and family when they lived in Cuba – from a friend.

He remembered the way to Javier's house like he'd been there yesterday, even though it had been over six months. It was just after four-thirty in the afternoon. He sighed with relief to find both cars gone from the driveway, and hurried to leave the envelope on the porch.

That done, he found a spot nearby to wait, hoping to catch a glimpse of his brother. At five-thirty, his brother's wife, Anna, pulled into the driveway. As she was getting the baby from the car, Javier pulled up in his car alongside hers. He hurried to her side and gave her a quick kiss, then happily took little Alejandro from her.

Ramos's heart tightened, and he watched them interact with a pang of envy. Before it took hold, a large wave of satisfaction replaced it. They were happy and healthy, and he couldn't have wished for more. Anna found the envelope and held it up for Javier to see. He gave Alejandro to her and read the message, then glanced up and down the street.

Ramos held his breath, afraid that Javier would spot him, but he'd picked his place well, and Javier's attention turned back to the envelope. He studied the message again, then, after another quick glance at the street, he followed his wife inside and closed the door.

Relieved, Ramos let out his breath, then started the car and drove away. Even if he didn't want to be part of their lives, it gave him comfort to know that Javier had the photos, and they wouldn't be lost or put away somewhere. With Javier, they would be treasured.

Ramos awoke the next day feeling more focused and alert. The sadness and melancholy that had dogged him for the last few days had retreated. He was ready to move on with his life and leave the past behind.

Restless, he spent the morning at the gym, then indulged in a full-body massage. After that, he picked up some new clothes to replace his shirt and blazer, along with a few other things that he liked.

Just as he got back to his room with his purchases, Sloan called. "Good news. I'll be there tomorrow in time for dinner. Let's meet at the Versailles Restaurant. It's one of my favorites, and they serve Cuban coffee. I'm already missing it."

"Sure," Ramos agreed, even though he didn't want anything to do with Cuba. "What time?"

"I should be there by six-thirty or seven. I'll text you when I get closer."

"Okay. I'll meet you there."

"I've got some great news!" Her voice bubbled with enthusiasm. "I'm back on track with the agency. In fact, they're giving me back my lead status. Getting that device was huge, and it's all because of you. I feel a little guilty that you're not getting the recognition for the part you played, but I'm sure it's not something you'd want."

"You're right about that," Ramos said.

They spoke for another minute before disconnecting, and Ramos shook his head at the irony. By blowing up the weapons in Mexico, it was his fault that she'd lost her privileges in the first place. Now she had them back because of him.

Didn't that mean she still owed him a favor? Hell, she owed him a lot more than a favor. And if it ever came up, he wouldn't hesitate to make sure she knew how big of a debt it was.

Having that much leverage over her put him in a good mood. There was no way she could top it, and he hoped it would keep him beyond her reach for a long time. Ready for a break from all his worries, he drove to the club and got there just before the big crowds.

The club manager's face turned pale to find Ramos entering through his door. It bolstered Ramos's confidence that he had that effect. He reassured the manager that he was just passing through, but he did it in a way that said otherwise. It was enough to get the royal treatment, and he spent the rest of the evening in good company.

He slept in the next morning and was just sitting down to breakfast when his phone buzzed. He picked it up, surprised to see that it was Manetto. Was something wrong?

"Ramos, sorry to bother you, but something's come up," Manetto began. "It's Shelby."

His gut clenched. "What's happened?"

Manetto sighed. "While we've been gone, Blake's been busy. He talked Shelby into going to Paris with him. I told her not to go, but Blake helped Chris with something, and now she's going with him. They left this morning, and I just can't shake the feeling that she might be in trouble."

Ramos could hardly believe that Blake Beauchaine was back in Shelby's life. He was a government agent who wanted her help, and Ramos couldn't shake the feeling that she was now in the same boat that he'd just gotten out of.

"I totally get that," Ramos agreed. "She's always getting into trouble. Do you have any idea what Blake wanted her to do? He hasn't found out about her ability, has he?"

"No. He only thinks that she has premonitions," Manetto said. "But that's enough. All I know is that he's meeting with a guy who was blacklisted from the agency, and he wanted Shelby to be there. I guess to help him know if the guy's telling the truth, or if he has something up his sleeve."

"That can't be good," Ramos said.

"I know. Listen, how would you feel about a trip to Paris?"

A slow grin spread across his face, and his stomach relaxed. "I think that's a great idea."

"Good. I'd feel better if you were there. Can you leave today?"

"Of course."

"I'll have Jackie book you on the next flight out of Miami and call you with the information."

"Sounds good," Ramos agreed.

Manetto let out a breath. "Thanks Ramos. You don't know how much better that makes me feel. Keep me posted, and make sure you both come back in one piece."

"I will." They disconnected, and Ramos shook his head. Shelby in Paris? What was she thinking? Her ability wouldn't help her much if she didn't speak French. And he was pretty sure she didn't.

As he finished up his breakfast, Jackie called about his flight. The plane left Miami at eight-ten that evening, but he'd need to be there at least two hours early. That meant he'd have to cancel his plans with Sloan.

Before he could decide if he was disappointed or not, he called her number. "Hey Sloan, it's me."

"Ramos. I'm glad you called. I might be able to come a little earlier."

"About that...I can't make it after all. Manetto needs me."

"But..." After a long pause, she sighed. "Are you sure?"

"Yeah."

"Does this mean you don't want to get together, or just that you can't right now?"

Ramos sighed and shook his head. "Sloan, look...it's better this way. I know you want something from me, but after what happened in Cuba, I can't do this...with you."

"I know that was a bad deal, but I promise it won't happen again. I meant what I said that I'd never ask you to help me. At least give me a chance to explain."

"Sloan...I can't."

"But...I just...I want to see you again."

Ramos closed his eyes. "I'd like to see you, too. That's the problem, because every time I see you I'm nearly killed. And when I'm not worried about that, I'm worried you'll find something to arrest me for."

Sloan didn't answer for a long time, and Ramos let the silence speak for itself. "You're right," she said, then she let out a big sigh. "But hey...can't a couple of friends share a drink sometime?"

Grateful for the reprieve, he huffed out a breath. "Sure. Besides, you owe me."

"For what?"

"For getting you back in the good graces of your boss. He may not know how much I did, but it's not something I'm likely to forget. So you're in my debt now."

"Hmm...I guess you've got a point. Just...don't get into too much trouble, all right? There's only so much I can do."

He chuckled. "Don't worry. I'm sure it won't be anything like Cuba or Mexico."

"That's true. Just think, without me around, you might get bored."

"I doubt that."

"Well, if you ever do..." She lowered her voice. "You know how to find me."

"Bye, Sloan."

"See you," she said, and ended the call.

Ramos slipped his phone into his pocket and glanced out the window. He smiled, relieved with how things had ended with Sloan. It was nice to have some leverage of his own for a change.

Maybe this whole trip to Cuba hadn't turned out so bad. He'd learned more about his family than he ever thought possible, so he was grateful for that.

Now he was ready to put it all behind him, and going to Paris to watch over Shelby was just the distraction he needed.

It didn't do any good to dwell on things he couldn't change. More importantly, he needed to put it somewhere deep in his mind before he met up with Shelby. He didn't need her feeling sorry for him, and he didn't want to feel that kind of pain in his heart.

Besides, he may not have a family like most people. But he had something else. He had Manetto, who was like a father to him, along with Jackie and Miguel who treated him like part of the family. Then there was Shelby. He knew she cared about him a great deal. They were his family now. They were all the family he needed. More important, he could trust them.

With renewed purpose, he paid for his food and left the restaurant. There were things he needed for the trip, but he had plenty of time to purchase them. Even though he didn't know what he was walking into, he was bound and determined to make sure Shelby had someone on her side, especially since he knew first-hand how important that was.

It was a role he'd played before, and the one he enjoyed the most. In fact, he'd never get tired of protecting Shelby. It gave him an excuse to keep her in his life and, even if it was the only way he could have her, it was enough.

Still, his heart raced just a bit to know he'd be in Paris with Shelby. How did that saying go? What happens in Paris stays in Paris?

He shrugged. He wouldn't do anything to ruin Shelby's life. But he could always dream.

DEVIL IN A BLACK SUIT

Hot and heavy Harley rolls down the street
Feel the vibrations on the ground beneath my feet.
Bright, light leather, chrome and steel
Pulling off his shades for a better view
I see eyes filled with fire and I know it's true.

I step up to his Harley caught up in his gaze,
Heart beating fast, and my head in a daze.
His fingers take my hand with an electric touch,
Sending little shivers through my body in a rush
Climbing on behind my arms hold him tight.
He smiles with pleasure 'cause he's won the fight.

Devil in a black suit staring at me,
Digging in my soul so I can't breathe
Devil in a black suit walking my way,
Pulling me closer my debts to pay
Babe, babe, babe...come on a ride with me.

Devil in a black suit looking at me
Digging in my soul so enticingly
Devil in a black suit holding out his hand
Pulling me closer like a regular man
Babe, babe, babe...come on a ride with me.
Come on a ride with me!

If you enjoyed *Devil in a Black Suit*, please consider leaving a review on Amazon. It's a great way to thank an author!

If you want to find out how Ramos and Shelby met, the first book in the series, *Carrots: A Shelby Nichols Adventure*, is available on Amazon and Audible

.

OR...to find out what happens to Ramos in Paris, here is a sample of the next book in the series.

THE NEXT SHELBY NICHOLS ADVENTURE
NOW AVAILABLE

DEVIOUS MINDS
By
Colleen Helme

(read on for a sample)

The first day of spring arrived, filling me with an overwhelming sense of freedom. Even though the temperature wasn't real warm, it meant that winter was officially over. Even better, a ride on the motorcycle behind Ramos was now a possibility.

I'd missed that and I'd missed him. He'd been gone for two weeks helping Uncle Joey take care of some out-of-town business. I wasn't exactly sure what that entailed and... believe me, I didn't want to know. Jackie, Uncle Joey's secretary and wife, told me they were both due back in the next few days, and deep down where I didn't want to admit it, I could hardly wait to see them again.

That probably made me a bad person, since I worked for Uncle Joey and he was a mob-boss. Ramos was his hit-man and he'd saved my life a few times. I had to admit, it was a far cry from the first time I'd met Ramos almost a year ago, when he was thinking he might have to kill me for the big boss.

I'd had to tell Uncle Joey my secret that I could read minds to stop that from happening. Since then, my skills had come in handy for Uncle Joey, and gotten me into a lot of trouble. But he'd always been there to bail me out, both literally and figuratively.

So now I helped Uncle Joey, not because I was forced into it, but because I wanted to. That was just twisted on so many levels, and he wasn't even my real uncle. But I couldn't seem to stop, so I did my best to keep on the right side of things.

Ramos was another part of that story. He was one hot and swoon-worthy man any woman would fall for. I had to keep reminding myself that I was happily married every time I laid eyes on him. He was the quintessential bad boy and, like a decadent chocolate dessert with whipped cream and a cherry on top, something that I might want in the worst way, but that would also be very bad for me.

If I wasn't married with kids...well, who knew what could happen, but I loved my husband and children, and Ramos respected that. Even so, there were still times when my heart seemed to have a mind of its own around him, and I'd have to rein it in or lose control, which was not an option.

Only a handful of people knew I could read minds, and I liked it that way. I told everyone else I had premonitions, and that mostly worked. I also had my own consulting agency, which included helping the police along with my own clients. Because of that, I managed to get into even more trouble, and that wasn't counting the mob-boss part.

Like now.

My husband, Chris, had asked for my help on a hard case. He was an associate partner in the prestigious law firm of Cohen, Larsen and Pratt. This case was the single most important event of Chris's career, mostly because the partners were looking to replace the Cohen part of the firm, and change it to Larsen, Pratt and...Nichols.

This was a huge deal, and I wondered if the fact that Chris handled all of Uncle Joey's accounts had something to do with it. Probably, but I wasn't touching that with a ten foot pole. This put a lot of pressure on me. Not as much as Chris, but still...I didn't want to screw it up for him.

That brought me to my problem. I wasn't sure I wanted to help Chris, mostly because he was defending a woman accused of killing her husband, and ten million dollars from the life insurance policy was in the balance. To complicate matters even more, the husband's company was one of Chris's biggest clients.

If they won, Chris's firm would get a nice, fat share, and also keep the company as a client. But from everything he'd told me, she sounded guilty as sin. If I listened to her thoughts, I'd know for sure, and that would just ruin everything. It made me realize that sometimes my 'gift' wasn't so great. Not when I had to use it to get someone off who actually deserved some jail time.

But...wasn't that what I did for Uncle Joey? So how was this any worse?

In fact, I'd recently made a deal with a government agent to keep Uncle Joey out of prison. In exchange for my help on one of his cases, he'd agreed to make any charges against Uncle Joey disappear. When Uncle Joey found out what I'd done, he wasn't too happy with me. Especially since he thought I'd told Blake Beauchaine I could read minds.

Once he knew I hadn't, and Blake just wanted me for what he thought were my mad interrogation skills, he'd calmed down. Still, Uncle Joey told me he could have handled anything Blake might have thrown at him without my deal. To be honest, it kind of hurt my feelings. Then he made me promise to involve him if Blake ever came to collect.

So now on top of everything else, I had Blake's phone call to look forward to, and Uncle Joey to involve after that. It was enough to give me an ulcer.

"Shelby? We're ready for you," Chris said, poking his head out of the conference room.

My stomach lurched, but I covered it with a quick nod and stood. Chris caught my reluctance and his mouth turned down on one side. I picked up his thoughts of disappointment that I was hesitant to help him, especially since I didn't seem to have the same qualms about helping Uncle Joey. What was up with that?

Before I could explain my misgivings, he pulled the door open, and I had no choice but to enter the room, knowing I'd just have to straighten him out later. The big honchos, Larsen and Pratt, stood to greet me, and I picked up their eager hope that, whether the client was guilty or not, I could help Chris win the case. Talk about pressure, and I hadn't even gotten started.

Then came the moment of truth, and Chris introduced me to his client. Her name, Victoria Hampton, sounded as rich as she looked, with her beautifully groomed, long brunette hair and dark eyes framed by long lashes and artful eyebrows. In her mid-forties, her hands were soft with manicured nails, and she wore a navy, tailored dress over her slim body with a matching set of cultured pearls and diamonds around her neck and hanging from her ears.

I could practically smell the money oozing off of her. Of course, without all that money, she wouldn't be out on bail, and it could have been a lot worse. Now her trial was about to start, and the fear in her eyes took some of the polish off her outward appearance.

"Nice to meet you," I said, not quite meaning it. "Thank you so much for helping us out," she answered, not only sincere, but desperate for anything that would get her out of this mess.

"Of course," I said. "Whatever you need."

While this made Chris happy, Victoria was ecstatic, and it changed her whole demeanor from desperate fear to quiet hope. She was thinking how Chris had told her I was their secret weapon, but until meeting me, she wasn't so sure.

Wow. I hadn't even done anything yet, and here she was, pinning all her hopes on me.

I listened closely and picked up that she was impressed with my credentials and no-nonsense attitude. She'd found out everything she could about me and my consulting agency. That brought her to my premonitions, and she wondered how they worked. Was there a chance I would find out the truth?

"Right...uh, Shelby?" Chris asked.

"Huh? Oh...sure," I said. I smiled and listened real hard to his thoughts, finding out that I'd just agreed to help them with the jury selection, which we'd discussed at home. Since they'd hired a jury selection specialist, I thought it was overkill, but I was still willing to help where I could.

I went back to Victoria's thoughts, but she wasn't thinking about who'd killed her husband anymore, so I'd missed my chance to know the truth about her... at least for now.

Of course, this was something Chris had given me strict instructions about, since he didn't want to know if she was guilty, so it was probably for the best. That also meant he didn't want me to listen too hard to her thoughts so I wouldn't know either. But how was I supposed to do that and help win the case? He'd said I was their secret weapon, but somehow he didn't want me to use my ability to hear the truth...or at least not tell him.

I sighed, knowing I was in an impossible situation. In all reality, I'd probably find out she was guilty and have to keep it to myself. I never had to do that with Uncle Joey. A big surge of resentment toward Chris hit me between the eyes. Oops... that wasn't good, so I pushed it away and focused on the discussion.

"I think we're ready to go," Chris said. "Do you have any questions, Shelby?"

"Yes," I said, coming to a decision. "Can I have a moment alone with Victoria?"

Chris' eyes widened, then his brows drew together. "Um...really? I didn't think..."

"I know what you thought," I said, tempering my words with a smile, "but I just need a minute, then I'll know the best way I can help her."

"Fine." He let out a sigh, resigned to the fact that I was going to do this my way. But he was thinking that I'd better not tell him she was guilty... even if it was the truth.

As they filed out of the room, I took a seat across from Victoria and smiled at her. "I'm sorry for your loss."

"Uh...thank you," she said, her eyes filling with sudden tears. She hadn't expected compassion. It reminded her that since her husband's death, she hadn't even had a chance to grieve. How unfair was that?

"This is so unfair," I began. "You lost your husband, and then on top of it, you're accused of his murder. I'm sure this has been a nightmare. Who would have thought something like this could happen?"

She sucked in her breath. "That's just what I was thinking."

"We'll figure this out, and I'll do everything I can for you."

"Thank you, Shelby."

"So tell me about that night." I'd already read the files, but I wanted to hear what she thought more than the words she spoke. Still, I took out my pen and the little notebook I used, then smiled and nodded at her to begin.

"Well... that night I went to bed early. Donovan and I had argued, and it had given me a headache, so I told him I couldn't talk about it anymore and was going to bed. The next morning I headed downstairs to the kitchen for a cup of coffee. I saw his feet first and knew something was wrong, so I ran into the room and...he was lying there, like he was asleep. If not for the blood, I would have thought he'd passed out or something."

She swallowed before continuing. "I hurried to his side and checked his pulse. I thought I felt something, but then I knew I was wrong because he was...so cold. I tried to wake him up anyway... I think I even tried to do CPR. Somewhere in the process, I got his blood all over me. After that, it's kind of a blur. I know I called nine-one-one and the police came with the paramedics.

"They asked me a lot of questions, but I don't even remember what they were, or what I said. I let them search the house for signs of a break-in, and they couldn't find anything. That's when it hit me that he must have killed himself. In my efforts to save him, I didn't even notice the gun. But the police did. They said it was in his hand, so it looked like he'd shot himself. It was the only thing that made sense, even though it was hard to believe. That's why I was so surprised when they came to arrest me."

She sighed and shook her head. "I didn't do it, but they said I had motive and opportunity." She caught my gaze.

"My husband had his faults, but I didn't kill him. I loved him."

"Do you really think it was suicide?"

"To be honest...it doesn't make sense that he'd kill himself, but I don't know how else to explain it. We argued, but his business is going great, and he had no signs of depression or anything like that." Guilt flooded over her as she thought of her last words to him, especially after she'd confronted him about his affair.

She'd threatened to divorce him and take him for all he was worth. She hadn't meant it, but she was hurting. That's when he'd reminded her of the pre-nuptial agreement she'd signed, and told her that if she went that route, she wouldn't see a dime of the money he'd made since the day they got married.

Right then, his betrayal had hurt so bad that she'd wanted to kill him. She'd gone to bed that night so upset that she couldn't sleep, so she'd taken a sleeping pill. She'd even thought of taking the whole bottle to kill herself, but couldn't go through with it. The next morning, he was dead. Part of her wondered if she'd done it in her sleep, but she knew she'd never left the bedroom. So how had it happened?

Whoa! She'd wanted to kill him, but didn't, and he'd ended up dead that very night? It sure didn't look like a coincidence. No wonder Chris was worried about winning this case. She looked guilty...but I was pretty sure she wasn't.

"I don't think you did it," I said.

"You believe me?" she asked, surprised.

"Yes. But the evidence... it looks bad, especially when you add his affair, the pre-nup and the threats of divorce into the equation."

She gasped. "But I haven't told anyone I threatened to divorce him."

"That's true," I said. "But with the pre-nup and the affair, it looks like you have an even bigger motive than the insurance money. Do you know the woman he was having the affair with?"

"No. In fact, I found out about the affair by accident. I'd gone to visit him at work. He wasn't expecting me because he was in a meeting, or so I thought. I sat in his chair behind his desk to wait and noticed that he'd left his laptop on with the browser open. That's when I saw the emails. They were pretty explicit and kind of made me sick." She sighed, thinking that was the worst day of her life, well... until she got arrested for murder.

"Did he know you'd found out?"

"Not until I confronted him that night. He didn't deny it, so even though I'd only seen the emails, I realized it had to be true."

"Do you have any idea who it is?" I asked again. "Could it be someone from work?"

"That's what I'd guess, but I don't know for sure. She signed them 'Aphrodite,' so it could be anyone."

"Damn," I said. "How much of this does Chris know?"

"He knows about the pre-nup and the affair. That's why he was so worried. But he thinks I only found out about the affair after Donovan's death, and I'd like to keep it that way."

"So, Chris doesn't know you threatened to divorce Donovan?"

"That's right," she said.

"Well," I sighed, "it might not matter now. If the prosecution finds the woman in question, or even someone who knew about the affair, they wouldn't hesitate to put them on the stand. They'll insinuate that your argument that night was about the affair. Who knows? They could even say Donovan might have asked you for a divorce, and since the pre-nup left him with all of his earnings, you snapped and killed him."

"I know how it looks. But I didn't do it," she said. "You have to believe me." Her eyes glittered with tears, and my heart broke for her. I remembered that feeling myself, since I'd been accused of a murder I didn't commit. My stomach clenched just thinking about it. I knew I had to help her and get to the bottom of this, or I'd never forgive myself.

"I do believe you. I just don't get it. He must have killed himself...unless...can you think of anyone who might have wanted him dead?"

"I honestly don't have any idea," she said, her shoulders drooping with defeat. She was hoping for a miracle before the trial started, but it didn't look like that was going to happen.

"Tell me about his company and the people he works with."

She sniffed with despair, thinking she'd done this a hundred times already, and they'd discovered nothing new. But maybe I could get something out of it no one else had. "Donovan owns an investment company. He and his partner buy up small companies and make them profitable. Donovan has always had a knack for making money. It seemed like everything he touched turned to gold."

"What about his partner? Do you think he might have killed him?"

"No, never," she said. "Chase took care of all the details, but it was Donovan who made the money. Chase would never do anything to jeopardize the company, and Donovan was the company's main asset. In fact, I'm not sure how Chase is going to manage without him."

"Could you call Chase and let him know I'd like to talk to him?" I asked. "I'd also like to talk to as many employees as possible."

"Um...sure, I guess." Her inquisitive gaze caught mine, and she wondered if this had something to do with my premonitions.

"I'm sure you're wondering about my premonitions and how they work," I said. Her mouth dropped open in surprise, and I couldn't help the grin that spread over my face. "Let's just say that talking to as many people who were involved in your husband's life as I possibly can, will go a long way to helping me know who killed him."

"Oh, okay. Good."

"Can you think of anyone else I should talk to?"

"No," she said, shaking her head. "I'm sorry."

"That's okay...at least I have a good place to start." I stood and smiled reassuringly. "I'm going to do my best to find out who did this, okay? Don't give up."

Relief flooded over her, and she blinked hard to keep the tears from her eyes. "Thank you, Shelby."

"You bet. I'll head on over to the offices right now."

"Oh, yeah...I'll call and let them know you're on your way."

"Thanks." I hurried out into the hall and ran right into my husband's chest. It was a nice chest, so I didn't mind too much. "Chris! What are you doing?"

"Waiting for you," he said, grabbing my wrist and pulling me toward his office. "We need to talk in private."

"You know I could break your arm right now if I wanted to, right?" I had been taking Aikido just for situations like this. Although, in Chris' case, I didn't really mean it.

"Honey," he grumbled, dropping my wrist and opening the office door. "This is serious." He closed the door behind me. "So...did you find out?" His piercing gaze caught mine, and his brows drew together.

I nodded, but kept my mouth shut.

After a moment, he threw his arms up. "Well? Are you going to tell me?"

"I thought you didn't want me to," I answered, hiding a smirk.

He huffed out a breath. "Shelby...forget that. If you know...it's probably better if I know too. It won't change anything. We'll still go with what we've got, but it might make a difference in how we proceed." He was thinking she was probably guilty, but he'd still do his best to present a fair case.

"Chris...she's innocent, but..."

"What? Really? She is?"

"Yes. But it's worse than you think. The argument they had that night was about the affair. Victoria threatened to divorce him. Does the prosecution know about the pre-nup?"

"Uh...yeah."

"If they find the woman he had the affair with..."

"I know Shelby, that's why I wanted your help." Chris sighed, but otherwise held himself together.

"Wow," I said, shaking my head in dismay. "This is bad. She looks guilty, but she's not. Are you sure he didn't kill himself?"

"Unfortunately, from all the forensic evidence gathered at the scene, they're saying he couldn't have pulled the trigger himself, and that someone else killed him and tried to make it look like a suicide."

"Bummer."

Chris shook his head, thinking of a lot worse words in his mind. Then he glanced at me with raised brows, knowing I'd heard every four-letter word he'd thought. I just shrugged. "It's okay. I thought a lot of the same words too. Anyway, it looks like I've got to find the real killer, so I'm headed over to her husband's investment company."

"Wait. What about the jury? You're supposed to help us pick them out."

"I know, but this is more important. Don't worry, you've gone over everyone with your specialist, so you'll do great. Oh...wait..." My brows drew together as I picked up his thoughts. "You're not worried about that. It's the partners. How come?"

"You said you'd be there to help. They're kind of expecting that."

"Are they both going?"

"Well...no," he said. "Larsen is, but that doesn't matter since I told them you'd be there."

"Oh...well, just tell them I've got a good lead on the real killer, and I'm following up on that right now. That should make them happy."

His breath caught. "You do? Why didn't you tell me?"

Oops. "Uh...honey...I was speaking hypothetically. I'm sure I'll know who it is after I talk to everyone. Right?"

Chris groaned. "Shelby." He was thinking that I exasperated the hell out of him, but in a good way...most of the time. He'd added the 'good way' part in case I was listening, but it didn't block out his other thoughts of how he'd have to lie to the partners to excuse my absence, and he didn't like it one bit.

I clamped my lips together before I could say *welcome to my world*, like I was thinking. I mean, I was doing him a favor, right? I tried not to be too upset and cut him some slack, since it wasn't easy for him to be married to someone who could hear his every thought. I knew I wouldn't like it much. The elevator dinged and I got in. "I'll call you."

"Yeah...or just come to the courtroom as soon as you're done, and try to hurry, since you might still be able to help. We're on the third floor, courtroom B."

"Okay." The door slid shut, leaving me in blessed silence. I closed my eyes and enjoyed it. Most of the time the noise didn't bother me too much; then when I couldn't hear anyone, like now, I realized how invasive those thoughts had been all along.

Ever since I'd been shot in the head at the grocery store, and ended up with my mind-reading ability, I'd harbored a small fear that I'd wake up one morning and find it gone. After nearly a year of reading minds, it had become like second nature to me. If I ever lost that ability, it would probably feel like losing an arm or a leg, and I hoped it never happened, even if it got me into more trouble that it was worth. How crazy was that?

END OF SAMPLE.
Devious Minds: A Shelby Nichols Adventure
is available in both print and kindle formats.
It's also available on Audible.

Newsletter Signup
Sign up for my newsletter at www.colleenhelme.com and get a FREE e-book of Catering to Murder, A Shelby Nichols Novella. By signing up you will receive news and information about new book releases and book deals in this series.

ABOUT THE AUTHOR

USA TODAY AND WALL STREET JOURNAL BESTSELLING AUTHOR

As the author of the bestselling Shelby Nichols Adventure Series, Colleen is often asked if Shelby Nichols is her alter-ego. "Definitely," she says. "Shelby is the epitome of everything I wish I dared to be." Known for her laugh since she was a kid, Colleen has always tried to find the humor in every situation and continues to enjoy writing about Shelby's adventures. "I love getting Shelby into trouble...I just don't always know how to get her out of it!" Besides writing, she loves a good book, biking, hiking, and playing board and card games with family and friends. She loves to connect with readers and admits that fans of the series keep her writing.

Made in the USA
Middletown, DE
08 August 2021

45632119R00151